# THE
# RELUCTANT HERO
### And the Massachusetts 54th Colored Regiment

## Richard Andersen

**Winston-Derek Publishers, Inc.**
Pennywell Drive—P.O. Box 90883
Nashville, TN 37209

Copyright 1991 by Winston-Derek Publishers, Inc.

All rights reserved. No part of this book may be reproduced in any form without written permission from the publishers, except by a reviewer who may quote brief passages in a review to be printed in a newspaper or magazine.

First printing

Andersen, Richard, 1946–
  The reluctant hero and the Massachusetts 54th Regiment / Richard Andersen.
    p.   cm.
    ISBN: 1-55523-392-9 : $10.95
    1. United States--History--Civil War, 1861–1865--Participation, Afro-American--Fiction. 1. United States. Army. Massachusetts Infantry Regiment, 54th (1863–1865)--Fiction. 3. Shaw, Robert Gould, 1837–1865--Fiction.  I. Title.
PS3551.N349R45   1991
813'.54--dc20
                                                            90-71334
                                                                CIP


PUBLISHED BY WINSTON-DEREK PUBLISHERS, INC.

Printed in the United States of America

For Helene Hinis

Had she been there, things might've been different.

Also by Richard Andersen

Fiction

Muckaluck

On the Run: The Fabulist Story of Felix Carvajal

Straight Cut Ditch

Non-fiction

Arranging Deck Chairs on the Titanic:
Crises in Education

Robert Coover

The Red Aristocrats:
A Biography of Michael and Catherine Karolyi

The Write Stuff:
A Practical Guide to Style and Style Mechanics

William Goldman

Writing that Works:
A Practical Guide for Business and Creative People

The American Negroes are the only people in the history of the world, so far as I know, that ever became free without any effort of their own. The Civil War was not their business, they had not started the war nor ended it. They twanged banjos around the railroad stations, sang melodious spirituals, and believed that some Yankee would soon come along and give each of them forty acres of land and a mule.

—W. E. Woodward
Civil War Historian

The physical difference between our races is a great disadvantage to us both. Your race suffers greatly by living among us, while ours suffers greatly from your presence. There is an unwillingness on the part of our people, harsh as it may be, for you colored people to remain with us. I do not propose to discuss this. It is a fact with which we have to deal. It is better for us both, therefore, to be separated.

—Abraham Lincoln

The eyes of thousands will look upon what you do tonight. You must prove yourselves or die in the attempt.

—Robert Gould Shaw

# I
# Boston

ROBERT GOULD SHAW WAS BORN INTO MONEY. Lots of it. And his parents knew what to do with it. They contributed to the arts and the library, supported scientific research, and gave considerable sums to charity. They also involved themselves in the crusade against slavery. By 1837, the year Robert was born, the Shaw's house at 44 Beacon Street had become a hotbed of abolitionist activity. Prominent Bostonians such as Wendell Phillips, William Lloyd Garrison, and Ralph Waldo Emerson plotted in the parlor, while escaped slaves in the basement prepared for their next stop on the Underground Railroad.

But it wasn't always like that. Francis Shaw's great uncle had fought in the Revolution and afterwards became the young nation's first consul at Canton. His descendants, however, quickly became more interested in profits realized by the China trade than social causes. They made their share of donations to respectable organizations but, on the whole, they were more concerned with enjoying the world than shaking it.

Not Sarah Shaw. The world had shaken her, and she wanted to shake it back. The daughter of a distinguished merchant who had worked his way up Boston's ladder of respectability, Sarah personified all her father had taught her about having her own way. There was nothing she couldn't accomplish once she set her mind to it.

Francis Shaw had learned in school that slavery was unjust, and he felt sorry for the poor Blacks who produced the cotton that kept his family's textile mill running, but he didn't feel bad enough to do much about it. When he suggested his family divest their manufacturing interests into something more respectable, his father asked him how willing he was to give up his comfortable home for the sake of a few hundred slaves whose condition would remain the same regardless of who owned the mill. Francis admitted he enjoyed living on Beacon Hill and wrote off slavery as another of the world's necessary evils. He kept attending abolition meetings, however. Sarah Shaw was a lot easier to listen to than his father.

Sarah knew from somewhere deep within her that slavery was an outrage. When she found out *her* father had investments that depended on the cotton trade, she refused to set foot in his house until the stocks were sold. Several days later, Mr. Sturgis was in the railroad business.

But that wasn't good enough for Sarah. Trains carried cotton, didn't they?

Mr. Sturgis asked for time. He had lost a lot of money selling his textile stocks so quickly.

He got forty-eight hours. On the forty-ninth, Sarah picketed his office with her anti-slavery group. One of the pickets was a young man named Francis Shaw. By the time Mr. Sturgis got himself into real estate, Francis and Sarah were in love.

Sarah ignited a flame in Francis' heart that surprised everyone who knew him. Almost overnight, he changed from an interested member of the movement into one of its firebrands and, as his and Sarah's involvement in the crusade grew, so did their affection. The three—Francis, Sarah, and the Cause—became inseparable. Together they made Francis' family realize that if they were not actively fighting slavery, they were supporting it.

When they married, Francis and Sarah were given a large share of their parents' investments. Rather than waste any of the money on a honeymoon, however, they moved into the Sturgis house on Beacon Street and began turning their dividends into action.

Their first venture was to change their basement into a hiding place for escaped slaves. The two children born to the Shaws knew about the abolition movement, but they had no idea they were living over a station on the Underground Railroad. Secreting slaves to Canada was illegal, and the Shaws thought it better if Annie and Robert didn't know their parents were criminals.

But there was more to the Shaws' involvement than the Underground Railroad. They spent a good part of their time converting Boston Brahmins into abolitionists and, in 1830, they helped publish the nation's first abolitionist newspaper: *The Liberator*. William Lloyd Garrison was its first editor.

Not everybody appreciated the Shaws' efforts, however. Mill owners feared growers in the South would believe the radical views expressed in *The Liberator* were widely held and would retaliate by cutting their cotton supply to Massachusetts. The workers knew what that meant: no jobs.

And who was responsible for this threat? Not the Blacks. They were minding their own business until the abolitionists put ideas into their heads. It was the rich! The ones who didn't know what it was like to support a family. The ones who had so much money they could afford to be liberal and high-minded. The ones who had nothing better to do with their time than cause trouble for the people who had made them wealthy in the first place. Well, workers had their rights too, and, by God, they were going to protect them.

William Lloyd Garrison was alone in his office when he heard a knock at the front door. Thinking it was Ralph Waldo Emerson, he went to let him in but, by the time he got there, the door was gone. Torn off its hinges by a mob of angry workers. Streaming into the press room, they began destroying everything in sight.

"What's the meaning of this?" Garrison shouted.

The workers paused. They hadn't expected anyone to be in the building. Now there was a witness.

Garrison's eyes revealed the contempt he held for people who forced their way onto other people's property. "You have no right to be here," he said.

"You're wrong, Mister," answered the mob's leader. "We've got every right to keep you from taking the food out of our children's mouths."

Garrison wondered what the man could possibly be talking about. But not for long. A rope was tossed around his neck and he was dragged out into the street.

Garrison screamed for help, but a blow to the face quickly silenced him. The workers began dragging him from one side of the street to the other while they looked for a lampost. Garrison had all he could do to keep from choking.

When the workers thought Garrison didn't have much longer to live, they threw him into a vacant lot about six feet below the street.

But Garrison had fooled them. Drawing on a strength he never knew he had, he rose to his feet, took the rope off his neck, and ran for his life.

While the crowd poured in after him, Garrison ran for the embankment on the other side of the street. As he reached the top, however, he was thrown back into the lot by a group of drunk sailors who happened to be passing by.

There was no escaping the mob now; they hadn't appreciated the editor's playing possum; this time there would be no mistake.

Garrison faced the workers.

A woman broke from the ranks to club him with a large piece of wood. While Garrison dodged her blows, the crowd stepped back to enjoy the macabre dance that followed. They weren't entertained for long. From the corner of his eye, Garrison saw a stone flying toward him. He deflected it with his arm, but the ones that followed were too much for him. He couldn't defend himself against the rocks *and* the club. Every time he was hit, the workers cheered. A man stepped out of the crowd and lifted Garrison onto his shoulders. "I'm going to drown him," he told the workers as he carried Garrison to a mud-hole at the far end of the lot. "Drown him! Drown him!" the mob shrieked in delight. "Drown him!"

The man flung Garrison head first into the water. His face struck a rock, and the full force of his body followed, snapping his neck. Those who hadn't hit, kicked, or stoned him were now called on to do their share. Garrison used the lull to gain his feet and stagger toward the middle of the hole. The mob raced around to the other side to head him off. By the time they got there, Garrison had reached the top of the embankment. "Save my life!" he cried to the first passing carriage.

The door opened and a large hand reached out to him. "To my church," a voice told the driver. "Quickly!"

While Garrison lay on the floor of the carriage, a handkerchief began wiping the blood from his face. Several minutes later, Ralph Waldo Emerson realized whom he had rescued.

The preacher was shocked. Like so many Boston liberals, he had insulated himself within a circle of friends who shared his views. It never dawned on him that his anti-slavery sentiments could drive anyone to violence. And who knew where it would end? If anyone recognized him helping Garrison into the carriage, his house might be attacked. His church could be burned. He had a wife to consider. Terrified by the possibilities, he brought Garrison to a hospital and thought seriously about getting out of town.

Garrison wasn't so easily intimidated. Within a month he was back on the street. And so was *The Liberator*. But from now on only the paper's workers knew where the press was located. This included Francis and Sarah Shaw who, over the next ten years, perfected their dual life. On the surface, they weren't much different than their neighbors. They had money, respectability, and two lovely children. Everywhere else, however, they were up to their necks in hideouts, secret agents, and guns.

# II
## West Roxbury

IN 1842, THE SHAWS BOUGHT A LARGE FARM IN WEST ROXBURY. Mr. Sturgis' health was failing, and they believed they could better care for him, raise their two children, and carry on their abolition work in an isolated country home.

Their only neighbors were the writers, artists, and musicians who lived in George Ripley's commune. Ripley had been an abolitionist and close friend of the Shaws for years but became disillusioned with their cause after the attack on Garrison. It had taught him a lesson: people with unpopular ideas get hurt.

Ripley's solution was to create a community where people with similar views could work together for their own common good. No religion was practiced, and ambition—which Ripley believed to be the cause of all that was wrong with the world—was not tolerated. Nor was there any deviation from what the majority decided was best for everyone. Ripley called his utopia Brook Farm.

Brook Farm included some of the age's best minds and talent. Nathaniel Hawthorne lived there with his new wife, Sophia Peabody. So did Charles A. Dana and John Sullivan Dwight. Henry David Thoreau and James Russell Lowell never lived there, but they visited regularly. For Ralph Waldo Emerson, who still hadn't gotten over the attack on Garrison, West Roxbury was too close to Boston. He settled in Concord.

Ripley wanted the Shaws to live in the community, but they had no interest in the required farm chores and didn't want to implicate innocent people in their illegal work. In addition to helping runaway slaves, they'd hired secret agents to infiltrate plantations and help other slaves escape. They'd also sent guns and ammunition to a radical named John Brown. Brown, who believed that the slaves would be freed only by the sword, had raised an army of abolitionists to prevent slaveholders from settling in the Kansas Territory. If Kansas was gong to enter the Union, Brown was going to make sure it went in as a free state.

Five-year-old Robert Shaw, of course, knew nothing of these things. His life really was a utopia. Especially in the summer and especially at Brook Farm. His cousin, Harry Sturgis Russell, lived there, and the two boys frequently followed George Ripley as he milked the cows, stored hay in the barn, and worked in the fields. "Fourteen years a Unitarian minister and I never felt closer to God," he once told Robert and Harry. Neither did they. Brook Farm was a constant round of activity, and the two friends participated in everything from picking apples to taking music lessons.

As Ripley had planned, the community's members did farm work in the morning and dedicated their afternoons to individual projects. Evenings were reserved for a concert, lecture, reading, or lessons in philosophy, mathematics, astronomy, Greek, and German. On Sundays, the members danced, held picnics, rowed boats on the Charles River, or went to Boston to shop. As Nathaniel Hawthorne put it, Brook Farm was "essentially a daydream, and yet a fact."

It was also an archetypal American experience. Like the Pilgrims who left Europe to discover the Bay Colony of Massachusetts, the people at Brook Farm invested all they had to launch their little community. In the words of their founder, "We have stepped off the weary treadmill of the established system and flown the ill-conceived coup that contains it. We have divorced ourselves from individual pride and supplied the principles of brotherhood in its place."

They also relied on donations from the Shaws and Emerson.

Ripley originally wanted to call his utopia "Camelot." He had even built a Round Table where all the people in the commune would sit equally, but the members voted against it. It wasn't practical; it took up too much room. Ripley was disappointed that his table wasn't enthusiastically received, and the members had to remind him of his pledge to triumph by mutual agreement rather than individual might. As long as the community maintained for its foundation everything that was lacking in the outside world, no Lancelot would be able to destroy it.

As things turned out, "Camelot" probably would've been the better name. Working in the fields gave the members a tan, but the chores also sapped their creative energies. Hawthorne wasn't in the fields a season when he wrote Emerson: "My greatest fear is not that I shall fail to be a farmer but that I shall fail to be anything else. I've turned over more clods of dirt than I can count and not one of them has etherealized into a thought. My thoughts, on the other hand, are fast becoming clods."

Ripley had enough energy and donations to run Brook Farm by himself, but his great strength was also a great weakness. A true builder of schemes rather than a mere experimenter, he often allowed his enthusiasm for the commune to overwhelm his original idea of what it should be. He came to believe, for example, that because he had created Brook Farm he was the only one who knew how to make it work. It wasn't long before he began substituting selfhood for brotherhood, and what began as a regenerative community quickly deteriorated into a monument to Ripley. When his motion for a Round Table was defeated for the third time, he stormed out of the room. No longer able to tolerate anyone who didn't share his own fanatical vision, he began spending more and more time with the animals. The members of the commune, on the other hand, became increasingly dissatisfied with the difference between Ripley's theory of mutual agreement and the reality of his monomania.

Hawthorne was the first to pack his bags. Moving into Emerson's old manse in Concord, he wrote a novel about his experiences at Brook Farm. He called it *The Blithedale Romance*.

Others quickly followed Hawthorne's lead. Charles A. Dana accepted a professorship at Harvard, and John Sullivan Dwight went on to become a leader in Boston's music society.

Robert Shaw and Harry Russell were having too good a time

to notice much of this, however. The four years they lived in West Roxbury were the happiest of their lives, and they never tired of telling stories about the famous people they met there. Robert's favorite story was the time he saw George Ripley carrying a lighted candle in the middle of the day. When Robert asked him what he was doing, Ripley said he was looking for Brook Farm.

But Brook Farm was more than a source of amusement for the boys. It was also a tremendous learning experience. Robert's fascination with languages began with the Greek and German phrases Charles Dana taught him, and his affection for the tales of Washington Irving was first inspired by one of Hawthorne's ghostly readings. The boy's most pleasing influence, however, was John Dwight. His concerts and stories about Mozart made Robert as close to a fanatic as he would ever become. He even tried to please Dwight the same way Mozart at five had impressed the Austrian violinist, Wentzel. Unfortunately, Robert was no Mozart. He did learn to play the violin, however, and, when he was older, often went to great lengths to attend concerts featuring Mozart's music.

The Shaws supplemented their son's education at Brook Farm with the Miss Mary Peabody School. Known to everyone as "Grandmother Boston," Miss Peabody taught plights: the plight of the poor, the plight of the downtrodden, the plight of the homeless immigrant, the plight of the oppressed worker, the plight of the subjected slave. There was no end to them. Francis Shaw once told Sarah that if they hadn't created their own lessons for Robert and Annie to complete at home, their children would never have learned to add.

Forty years after Robert left Miss Peabody's school, Henry James satirized the teacher as Miss Birdseye in his novel *The Bostonians*. "Since the end of the Civil War much of her occupation was gone; for before that her best hours had been spent in fancying that she was helping some Southern slave to escape. It would have been a nice question whether, in her heart of hearts, for the sake of this excitement, she did not sometimes wish the Blacks back in bondage."

But this is an unfair statement. Even if Miss Peabody had loved only causes and languished only for emancipations she was no Miss Birdseye. Unlike the character James portrayed, Miss

Peabody did something about what troubled her. And Robert was not the only student she influenced. Several of the men he fought with in the Civil War—including Henry James' older brother Wilkie—never forgot the "life lessons" they learned from Miss Peabody.

Robert's most penetrating influence, however, was his grandfather. And what Mr. Sturgis did that impressed the boy was something very ordinary: he died.

"How old are you?" Grandfather Sturgis asked when Robert was brought in to see him for the last time.

"Eight, sir."

"Yes, well I had hoped to tell you this when you were older. Now I won't be able to. Do you understand why?"

"Because you're going to heaven."

"That's one way of putting it. Did your mother tell you that?"

"Yes, sir."

"I won't argue with her. I'll just tell you what I have to say and be done with it, but I want you to listen carefully because I'm not going to be able to repeat myself. Is that clear?"

"Yes, sir."

"Good. Now come close by and hold my hand. Look me straight in the eye. I mean every word I say, and I want you to mean every word you hear."

Robert nodded to show he understood.

"Someday you're going to be in the same position as I'm in. You're going to be lying on your back waiting for God to come and take you to heaven."

The boy's eyes filled with tears.

"Now stop that. What I have to say is more important than your feeling sorry for me. Someday, you're going to die, too, and, while you're waiting for the call, your life is going to pass before your eyes. Even this day will be as clear to you as it is right now. You're going to decide whether you've lived a good life or a bad one. If you do what I tell you, you'll be able to say you lived a good life. You'll be able to die at peace with yourself."

Robert dried his eyes.

"Most of the men in this world aren't *whole* men, Robert. They're only partly men. The rest of them is something else."

Already the boy was lost.

"Let me explain what I mean by a *whole* man. The world gives each man a job to do. Some men are farmers, some ministers, some teachers, and so on. Farmers farm, ministers minister, and teachers teach. As each man gets older, however, he often forgets who he is. He forgets who the person was that became the farmer, or the minister, or the teacher. He becomes a farmer, minister, or teacher instead of a *whole* man farming, a *whole* man ministering, or a *whole* man teaching. In other words, he becomes his job. He becomes interested in what the job will bring him. Usually this is money, but it doesn't have to be. It could be land, saved souls, minds that think the same way his does. Whatever. The farmer, minister, and teacher lose what made them *whole* in the first place. They may be good farmers, ministers, and teachers, but they're not all that they were. They're no longer *whole*."

Grandfather Sturgis knew from the glaze in Robert's eyes he'd lost him, but there was no time to repeat himself. He'd have to get through to the boy on one last try: "There was a time in my life, son, when I was a merchant. I had forgotten who I was when I was a *whole* man, when money and power weren't my only reasons for living. Your mother never forgot who she was, however, and one day she helped me remember the *whole* man who'd become a merchant. It took a while for me to get reacquainted with myself, but I did it, and I can tell you now that, thanks to your mother, I can look at my life and say the last part of it was good. If you ever need advice or help of any kind, go to her. She'll always help you remember who you are."

Robert said he would, but most of what his grandfather had said was beyond him. What's more, he didn't care. All he knew was that Grandpa was going away forever.

"Don't give up on me now, son," said Grandfather Sturgis when he saw the tears returning to Robert's eyes. I've already got one foot in the stirrup; this won't take much longer."

Robert did his best not to cry.

"Hold my hand tight and look me straight in the eye. We haven't much time. The best way to remember who you are is to always do what's right. Don't worry about the consequences. As long as you do what's right, you'll always be *whole*. There'll always be peace in your heart, and death will never frighten you. Being *whole* isn't easy, Robert. You may have to hurt people's feelings sometimes. Even the ones you love. But that doesn't matter. You must always do the right thing or die in the attempt."

# III
# NEW YORK

SHORTLY AFTER GRANDFATHER STURGIS DIED, the Shaws moved to Staten Island. Francis and Sarah had done just about all they could in New England; it was time to conquer new territory.

New York offered the biggest challenge as well as the greatest potential. Most of the city's immigrants favored slavery because they didn't want to compete with freed Blacks for the most menial jobs, but New York also had more free Blacks than any other city. The contributions they could make on behalf of their own people were enormous.

Sarah envisioned settling in Harlem, the only place in the whole country where the Underground Railroad wouldn't have to be underground. And how much more effective black agents would be than the white ones they'd hired! They could roam from plantation to plantation without arousing suspicion. Even a liberation army, like the one John Brown wanted to form, was possible.

But the Shaws weren't well received in Harlem. The people wondered why whites with money wanted to live with Blacks who didn't have any. The couple was suspected of being government agents sent to obtain a list of black leaders who could be arrested any time there was trouble in the community or a case the police couldn't solve. Besides, Harlem had no need for an

Underground Railroad. Escaped slaves came into the city every day; they were always taken care of.

Harlem didn't look all that attractive to the Shaws, either, once they saw it. There were a few decent houses, but most of the homes were overcrowded and run down. The people seemed that way, too. They laid about everywhere while the garbage in the streets piled up about them and the buildings edged closer to the day when they'd come tumbling down on their heads. Rotten vegetables and dead animals luxuriated like flower gardens. Sarah wondered why nobody bothered to pick up a broom. What was the matter with them? They were poor but did they have to be filthy? Francis thought the men looked like they could kill you simply because they had nothing better to do. Perhaps Harlem, with its poverty, insularity, cynicism, and suspicion, wasn't such a good idea after all.

But Staten Island was. Close enough to Harlem to make the necessary contacts, yet far enough away to enjoy the country life they'd come to love in West Roxbury, the Shaws' house overlooked Kill van Kull. From their veranda, they could see Robbins Reef Lighthouse and, beyond it, New York Harbor.

Robert felt sorry for the people in Harlem, but he was glad he didn't live with them. What could his parents have been thinking of? He asked his father, but the answer wasn't very satisfactory. Something about seeing how the other half lived and learning to appreciate the life you had. Robert didn't think it was necessary to live in Harlem to do that. Why didn't the Blacks move someplace else? There were plenty of nice places in Staten Island and Massachusetts.

The veranda from which Robert watched ships in the harbor was one of them. Inspired by the sea stories his father gave him, he imagined sailing all over the world. *Robinson Crusoe* was his favorite story, but most of the time he didn't care where any book took him as long as he got there by ship. Even *Of Plymouth Plantation* was good up to the chapter when the pilgrims landed on Cape Cod.

Staten Island as a whole, however, disappointed Robert. And not because there wasn't much to do; there just wasn't anybody to do it with. Missing his grandfather, Harry Russell, and the people at Brook Farm, he'd tried playing with his sister, but he had no interest in "House" and Annie wasn't very good at "Cowboy and Indian." Bored, frustrated, and alone, Robert turned to his mother.

Sarah wasn't an affectionate person, but she had a gentle way of encouraging the trust and confidence of others. Friends found themselves revealing their deepest feelings to her because she understood their problems and genuinely cared about helping them.

It was no different with Robert. Mourning the death of his grandfather and the absence of his friends, he wasn't interested in meeting new people. Sarah understood this and explained Grandfather Sturgis' death in words the boy could comprehend. She also helped Robert understand what his grandfather meant by a *whole* man. In other words, she gave her son's world a sense of order. It was her order, but it made him feel secure. Whenever anything bothered him, all he had to do was tell her. She'd understand and make it better for him. As Grandpa had said, she knew herself and would always help him remember who he was. She'd keep him *whole*.

Sarah's vision of the world was much like a giant china cabinet in which everything had its place. She wasn't familiar with every piece in the cabinet, but she knew all the principles that determined its order. For this reason, she could never be found at fault for anything she did.

As sound as Sarah's principles may have been, however, they were often blurred by a deep feeling of inferiority. The daughter of a wealthy merchant and not a real Boston Brahmin like her husband, Sarah couldn't admit that anyone had an advantage over her. Rather than look down on everybody with disdain, however, she pitied them. Of her friend Fanny Kemble, Sarah would say: "Fanny may be the most popular actress of her time and a devoted abolitionist, but she's divorced. No amount of fame or money can compensate for that." Maria Lowell, on the other hand, had money, fame, *and* a marriage but, "with a husband like James Russell Lowell, she won't be long for this world." And she wasn't.

Robert, of course, was too young to notice a pattern in his mother's observations and, dependent as he was on them to order his world, he unconsciously adopted many of her views without any of her accompanying social graces. In short, he became a snob.

But snobbery wasn't Robert's only problem. By the age of ten he'd become too close to his mother. Sarah knew from what had happened to David Thoreau what that meant: there was no longer any reason for Robert to do anything for himself. To put some distance between Robert and his mother, Francis and Sarah enrolled their son in St. John's Boarding School at Fordham.

Robert didn't want to leave, but Sarah convinced him he had to go if he wanted to remain *whole*. Shortly after arriving in the Bronx, he wrote: "The school is very pretty, but it's so old I could never like it. I wish you hadn't sent me here as I don't see myself returning after the first vacation. The place just isn't suitable."

Nor was Robert. Sarah was proud to be a Unitarian, proud of its contributions to the abolition movement, and proud to compare its record with those of other faiths. She expected no less from her son.

Robert hadn't completed his first class before he accused his fellow students of worshipping statues.

When Father O'Connor put his hand over his mouth to pretend to stifle a laugh, the rest of the class followed his cue and roared. Fighting the Holy War in the Bronx was going to be more difficult than listening to his mother on the veranda in Staten Island, but Robert wasn't about to give up. Every day he went to class hoping for an opportunity to land a blow for Unitarianism. Finally, he got one: Father O'Connor introduced the idea of the Holy Trinity.

Robert's hand shot into the air. How could there be such a thing as a Trinity if God never mentioned it in the Bible?

"The Bible isn't our only source of revelation," Father O'Connor replied. "If there was no Bible, you'd still believe in God, wouldn't you?"

"Yes, Father."

"Why?"

"Because everything in nature proves there's a God. Only a being greater than nature could have created it."

"Then if you don't need the Bible to prove that God exists, why do you think you need it to prove that there's a Trinity?"

"The Bible is God's word. If there was a Trinity, He would've said so."

"I don't know all that's in God's mind, do you?"

This made the class laugh and Robert retreat to what he knew.

He insisted that Father O'Connor show him somewhere in the Bible where God said there was a Trinity.

"Jesus mentions His Father in heaven several times, and He tells us that His Spirit will be with the Church He founded until the end of the world. These three—the Father, Jesus, and the Holy Spirit—make up the Trinity. The word isn't mentioned in the Bible because we've come to refer to the three beings in one as the Holy Trinity since the Bible was written. It's easier than repeating all three names every time we want to talk about them."

Robert had nothing to say about this and left the class feeling he had won a victory. Father O'Connor had admitted there was no mention of the Trinity in the Bible; his mother would be proud; soon he would go home.

Sarah congratulated her son on his triumph, but there was no mention of his going home.

Robert wondered what more he had to do to prove himself. When Father O'Connor introduced the subject of original sin, the boy leaped at another opportunity to please his mother. He demanded to know where in the Bible God said that unbaptized babies couldn't go to heaven.

Father O'Connor admitted God never said unbaptized babies couldn't go to heaven. The fate of unbaptized babies had been determined by the church fathers.

Robert was up two rounds to one. On the subject of redemption, he went for the knockout. "If Christ died for our sins," he jabbed, "then we're all going to heaven. That's what 'dying for our sins' means. We're all going to be saved when we die."

Father O'Connor was losing patience with the boy, but he wanted to be fair. He explained that Christ's death only opened the gates of heaven; it didn't guarantee we were all going to go through them. If what the boy said was true, why hadn't Jesus told both thieves they would be with Him in paradise?

Robert realized Father O'Connor had him on that one. And it was such a simple point, too! Why hadn't his mother realized it? Now he was stuck in front of the class; everyone was looking at him. "You said Christ died for our sins. 'Our' means 'us,' doesn't it?" Robert asked Father O'Connor.

"Yes, it does, but . . . "

"Thank you," Robert interrupted. "That's all I wanted to know."

The students looked at Father O'Connor to see what he would do. No one had ever been disrespectful to him. The Jesuit saw the expression on the students' faces and, without any emotion, took a piece of paper from his desk drawer, wrote something on it, and asked Robert to report to the headmaster. "There's a name for people like Robert," he told the class after Robert had left the room. "Can anyone tell me what it is? John?"

"Stupid."

"Robert's not stupid, John. Someone who's stupid doesn't know any better. Bryan?"

"A liar?"

"A kind of a liar, but not a *real* liar. Not someone who says false things to intentionally harm anyone. Robert thinks what he says is true. Michael?"

"A Protestant."

"Robert is a Protestant, Michael, but that's not quite the word I'm looking for. Does anyone else have any suggestions?"

They had plenty. None of them favorable and each one making an impression on every boy in the room. Finally, someone guessed the word Father O'Connor had in mind. Robert was a "heretic."

"Let us kneel and pray for his soul," the priest intoned.

Robert, meanwhile, was about to do some praying of his own. With Father O'Connor's note in one hand and a leather strap in the other, the headmaster was telling the boy: "My son, every person in this world has a right to his opinion. When we get into an argument and can't convince the other person of our point of view, we often say, 'You have your opinion and I have mine.' But some opinions, Robert, are wrong. Even if people have a right to hold them, they are still wrong. Your parents are abolitionists, are they not?"

"Yes, Father."

"What do you think they'd consider a wrong opinion?"

"The Trinity."

"I'm sure they would, but not because they're abolitionists. Wouldn't they think that to be in favor of slavery is a wrong opinion?"

"Yes, Father."

"Then you must know that in certain parts of this country your parents' opinion is wrong and being in favor of slavery is right."

"Slavery is wrong no matter where you are."

"My son, I'm not arguing with you about slavery. I'm about to punish you, and I want you to understand why."

"But I didn't *do* anything."

"You *think* you didn't do anything. That's why I want you to know why you're being punished. I don't want you to misbehave again."

"But I didn't misbehave once."

"Robert, your opinions may be correct in your home and in your church, but they are not acceptable here. Now that doesn't mean you don't have a right to them. You do. What you don't have is the right to express your opinions in ways that interfere with the education of your classmates."

"I disagreed with Father O'Connor. What's wrong with that?"

"Nothing, but that's not all you've done. Since you first walked into his class, you've continually interrupted Father O'Connor's lessons to challenge him with your points of view and then refused to listen to what he has to say. Now I know that's true because I've had the same experience with you today in this room. You say you're just stating your opinion. I'm telling you you're disturbing the class, and you refuse to listen."

"I listened to Father O'Connor, but he couldn't prove me wrong."

"That's because religion isn't based on proof, Robert, but on faith. Something that you have very little of and will someday regret. But today you're going to learn that you have a responsibility to the other students in your class, namely, not to disrupt their education."

"I wasn't. I was only saying my opinion. If Father O'Connor was a good teacher and Catholics had the best religion, I would've changed my mind. And what Father O'Connor said would've helped the other boys learn their religion better. But he couldn't prove I was wrong, so he sent me to you with a note that said I was bad, and now you're going to hit me for something I didn't do."

"You can tell yourself that, Robert, but you can't alter the fact that you've continually made yourself a center of attention by disrupting Father O'Connor's class. Well, now you're going to get the kind of attention you deserve. Put out your hand."

"But . . ."

"No more excuses, Robert. Put out your hand; take your punishment like a man."

Down came the strap. Robert's hand constricted with pain. Hot tears filled his eyes.

"Now the other."

Again the strap came down. Robert's fingers contorted above the burning sensation in the palm of his hand.

"First hand."

The boy couldn't believe he was going to be hit again. He'd never been beaten in his life. Just the thought of another blow sent tears rushing down his cheeks.

"First hand," the headmaster repeated.

The boy put out his hand; the strap made a wide arc above Father Ryan's head.

Robert flinched, and the strap came down on its side instead of flat on the surface of the boy's hand. There was blood.

"Go to the lavatory," the headmaster told Robert. "When the bleeding stops, you can go back to your class."

Robert ran to his room instead. In a letter to his parents, he begged to come home and, to demonstrate the urgency of his request, allowed drops of blood to fall in the margins and under his signature.

The Shaws were shocked that their son had been hit, but they refused to let him leave the school. Sarah congratulated him for being brave and standing up for what was right. "You're remembering who you are," she wrote. "Grandfather Sturgis is proud of you."

But the damage had already been done. Labeled a heretic, Robert became a butt for his classmates' practical jokes. Hardly a day went by when his pen wasn't stolen, his bed shortsheeted, or he didn't open a book to discover someone had spit between the pages.

Francis Shaw wanted to write to the headmaster, but Sarah wouldn't let him. "If we protect Robert from this adversity, he'll think he can run to us whenever he's in trouble."

"I thought that's what parents were for."

"He has to learn to be a man and stand on his own two feet."

"He's only ten years old."

"And where was Alexander the Great when he was ten?"

"Robert isn't Alexander the Great, Sarah."

"How do you know? This is the first time he's been on his own and the first difficulty he's encountered. If he can overcome this obstacle, the next one will be easier. And the one after that. By the time he's fifteen, who knows where he'll be?"

"Who knows if he'll make it to the end of the term? I think something should be done."

"Something will be."

Sarah sent her son a sketching kit but, by the time he got around to using it, someone had written "HERETIC" on all the pages of his pad.

Robert was on the next coach to Staten Island. Twenty-four hours later, he was back in his room at St. John's with a new sketch pad under his arm, his mother's words of approbation in his ears, and a renewed sense of determination on his brow. He had to stick it out until summer or die in the attempt.

Robert decided to stick it out, but events continued to conspire against him. When a student cheated off him during an exam, he was accused of giving answers. "I was innocent," he wrote his parents, "but that wouldn't have stopped the headmaster if he thought a beating would help me keep other people's eyes off my papers. I wish now he had beat me. I would've been so mad, I almost certainly would've run away."

"You have to show the headmaster, Father O'Connor, and everyone else in that school what you're made of," Sarah answered. "You're not going to do that by running away."

Nevertheless, Robert continued to fill his parents' mailbox with complaints. "Whenever I think of the way I'm treated here, I feel like crying, and sometimes I can't help crying before all the boys. St. John's is absolutely the worst place I've ever been. Worse than Harlem."

Four years later, the beatings, pranks, tears, and letters stopped. The Shaws were sailing to Europe. Robert was free at last.

# IV
## SORRENTO

IT WAS A ROUGH CROSSING. Just off the Azores, the sea rose, waves washed over the deck, and the sky came down so low Robert thought he could touch it. Sailors had to be tied to their stations; everyone else crawled about on their hands and knees. For five days, no passenger was allowed on deck.

This wasn't the life at sea Robert had envisioned from the family veranda on Staten Island. What had made his parents decide to cross the Atlantic in the middle of December?

They were frightened. Within the past few months, a spy had infiltrated the Underground Railroad, federal authorities had raided more than a dozen stations, and two of the Shaws' agents were in jail and talking. Plantation owners throughout the South vowed revenge. Helping runaway slaves was one thing, but sending agents to help them escape was going too far. Who did these abolitionists think they were? Preaching human decency on the one hand and stealing innocent people's legal property on the other!

Francis and Sarah got a letter saying that others could play their game. From now on, no abolitionist was safe. Nor were their children. The plantation owners were going to use the Shaws as examples of what happened to people who sent agents into the South.

Francis suggested taking the family abroad until the whole thing blew over.

Sarah's first choice was England. She believed the English were the most civilized people in the world because they'd liberated their slaves in 1833 and were wise enough to allow themselves to be governed by a woman. Sarah wished America was more like England.

Robert wasn't so sure. He found London big and confusing. The people sounded funny when they talked, and their words meant different things than they did in America. In Boston and New York, a street was a street, but in London a street could be a garden, a terrace, a park, a lane, a hill, a place, a crescent, a court, an inn, or a circus. And that was only the beginning! The people kept to themselves, the food was terrible, it rained almost every day, and, when the sun did come out, it only lightened up the sky enough for people to see where they were going.

The continuous sleet and dark skies also affected Sarah. She became haunted by fears of kidnapping, ransom, and violence. She even imagined a Southern agent trailing the family on Regent Street.

Francis tried to reason with Sarah, but her fears for Robert and Annie were beyond reason. England was no longer safe; they had to move on.

But everywhere they went, Sarah kept seeing spies and kidnappers. As a result, the Shaws never stayed in any one place for more than three days and, after seven months, Francis couldn't take it any longer. He refused to pack another bag. "We can't just wander around Europe forever," he told Sarah.

"We have the money."

"It isn't fair to the children."

"It's for their sakes that we're doing it. Do you think I enjoy living out of a trunk?"

"No, but the children should be in school. They're falling behind in their studies, and the more they stay out, the harder it's going to be for them when they return. How much longer do you think it will be before they suspect that this tour isn't just a vacation? How many children do you know who are taken out of school in the middle of winter to go traveling around Europe indefinitely? I say it's time to go home."

Sarah refused. As long as she had the slightest premonition of a tragedy, she wasn't going any closer to New York than Cherbourg. She also realized, however, that she wasn't helping the abolition movement much from her hotel room in Zurich, and she had to admit the constant traveling from place to place was wearing them all pretty thin. Eventually, she reached a solution: she and Francis would return to America; the children would remain in schools on the continent.

Robert and Annie were placed in the M. Roulet School at Neuchatel. Like St. John's, the school was Catholic, and Sarah insisted her children proclaim their Unitarian faith the moment they entered their first class. The boy agreed but, after his family left for home, he wrote: "I've changed my mind. You told me not to be afraid to declare my opinions. I'm not. I will say I am a Unitarian to anyone who asks, but I don't see how my challenging everyone as I did at St. John's does any good. It just brings up difficult discussions and, as I don't wish to be a reformer, apostle, or anything of that kind, I'll leave the business of converting others to you."

Because she didn't wish to give Robert a reason to run away from his new school, Sarah didn't question the boy's decision and he was able to enjoy his two years at Neuchatel.

It would've been hard not to. His room faced Mount Blanc, the students were of a similar background and temperament as himself, physical punishment was prohibited, and M. Roulet was an excellent teacher. Robert discovered he enjoyed reading French novels and the poetry of Byron. When he tried his own hand at "making some poems," however, he seldom got beyond the first line. He practiced simple Mozart pieces on the violin, sang in the choir, and learned to ski on the Jungfrau. He even made a friend, his first since Harry Russell at Brook Farm.

Robert met Heinrich during a game of hide and seek, and they quickly became friends. Heinrich said it was almost as if they had known each other before and were becoming reacquainted. That's how Robert felt, too. It was as if there had never been a time when he didn't know Heinrich. They went to class together in the morning, took walks in the afternoon, and shared their homework in the evening. When their roommates went home to visit their families, Robert and Heinrich spent the nights together, pretending they were Don Juan and talking about the women they'd someday love.

During the summer between terms, the boys traveled to Heinrich's home in Hanover. They went to *biergarten*, learned to smoke thin cigars, and became obsessed with every *fraulein* they met.

The following summer, Robert and Annie joined their parents in Sorrento. Francis and Sarah were on another forced vacation and had rented a villa to serve as an Underground Station for abolitionists whose lives were in danger in the States. Two days after Robert arrived, the vision he and Heinrich had fantasized about walked through the front door. Only Fanny Kemble wasn't on "vacation"; she was on tour. Her life wasn't in danger; it was in demand.

Robert hadn't seen Fanny since before he'd sailed with his family to England. That was almost three years ago. He was only a child then. Now Fanny would meet Robert Shaw the man, or almost a man.

Robert remembered when Fanny used to come to their house on Staten Island for dinner. He'd been struck by her beauty even then, but there was more to Fanny Kemble than beauty. That was certainly a part of it—she hadn't become the most famous actress in America on just her talent—but there was something else. It had to do with the way she moved and smiled and touched people on the arm whenever she spoke to them. Perhaps it was the touch he liked so much. It made him feel cherished and secure. Now he wanted to touch back, but he had to be careful. He was only fifteen, and his parents didn't know how much he'd changed over the past two years. If they suspected he liked Fanny for any reason other than her work in the anti-slavery crusade, he'd be on the first train back to Neuchatel. Thank God for the abolition movement! It was the only reason why his mother had allowed Fanny to become her friend in the first place. She was, after all, divorced, and it didn't help that she was an actress. He once heard Mrs. Lowell tell his mother that Fanny never got off the stage; Mrs. Hawthorne said she lacked a certain refinement.

Robert didn't care. Fanny made everybody else seem stuffy. Now that he thought about it, he wondered if his mother's friends were jealous because they couldn't be like Fanny.

When Fanny saw Robert, she kissed him on the cheek, held him by the shoulders, and said she was shocked by how much he had grown. She never would've recognized him. When he left New York he was a boy. Now he was a man.

Robert felt like he'd died and gone to heaven. Not almost a man, or practically a man, or in a few more years a man, but a man. What a wonderful woman Fanny was! How he hated Mrs. Lowell!

Robert told Fanny it was good to see her again and ran out the door. Within minutes, he was back with a tray of gaudy Italian pastry and a pot of insufficiently steeped tea.

Never suspecting Robert might be romantically interested in a woman, let alone someone more than twice his age, the Shaws silently congratulated themselves on having sent their son to the M. Roulet School. His manners had never given them any reason to complain, but he'd never done anything like this, either. It was almost worth suffering through the tea and pastry. And that wasn't all. Before Fanny left, Robert offered to give her a tour of Sorrento. He hadn't even been to the *Marina Piccola!*

Fanny said she'd love to go. As an actress and a divorced woman, she'd learned the hard way how important it was to feel accepted. Most people considered her a threat to the moral stability of their homes, and a list of her friends revealed that, except for husbands who wanted to run away with her, just about everyone else was either too old to care about conventions or too young to know about them. Theatre people accepted her, of course, but Fanny didn't like them. They were always calling attention to themselves. She sometimes wondered whether the Shaws had learned to tolerate artists when they lived near Brook Farm or if they appreciated all the work she did for the abolition movement, but most of the time she was just happy to be with a family she didn't threaten.

Robert told Fanny everything he could think of to say about himself within the first few minutes of their tour, and he only lasted that long because she had asked him questions about what he'd said. When it was her turn to talk, she didn't say anything. For what seemed like a week they walked the streets of Sorrento without uttering a word.

Robert blamed himself for being such a bore. He had to be

crazy to think Fanny would find him attractive. "Why haven't you said anything about your life?" he finally blurted out. "I've told you everything there is to know about mine."

Fanny apologized. She hadn't realized she was being rude. It was just that Robert's life was so interesting; hers seemed dull by comparison.

Robert was flattered. He led Fanny through a deserted park overlooking the Bay of Naples. They could see Mt. Vesuvio, and there was an intense feeling of summer in the air. Not peaceful, but hot and restless. As they walked farther into the park, the trees became more and more dense, the flowers less dry and brittle. "Isn't it lovely?" Robert asked.

Fanny nodded. The heat had made her lightheaded. She could feel drops of moisture running down her back. The trees acted as a shield against the sun, but they also prevented the heat from escaping. Everything hung around them like overripe fruit.

"You look pale," Robert said. "Are you all right?"

"Yes. It's just that this park is so enchanting. Did you know Odysseus was just off the coast of Sorrento when he tied himself to a mast so he could listen to the call of the Sirens? That's where the word 'Sorrento' comes from: 'Sirens'."

They had stopped walking and were looking at each other.

Suddenly, Robert grabbed Fanny as if she was one of the girls Heinrich had introduced him to in Hanover. He could feel the perspiration under her blouse as he drew his body close to hers. He rubbed her back, gently at first, then more violently. His face, drenched in sweat, sought hers. Everything depended on that first crucial kiss. She had to know how much she meant to him.

"Oh, dear," Fanny exhaled when they finally separated.

Robert jumped back and apologized.

"Don't be sorry," Fanny told him. "That was a wonderful surprise. One of the nicest I've known."

"Really?"

"I wouldn't say it if it wasn't true."

"You know you've always been special to me," Robert said.

"Really?"

"I wouldn't say it if it wasn't true."

Fanny laughed.

Robert tried to kiss Fanny again, but her hand kept him from getting close to her. "Dearest child," she said.

"You said I was a man."

"You are, but I've known you since you were a child, and now you're a man. You're like two different people: an old friend and a new one."

"I've always loved you, Miss Kemble. Ever since I was little, but I couldn't tell you because I thought you'd laugh at me. Now I'm a man, my love is a man's love, too. Can't we kiss again?"

"I don't think so."

"We did before."

"I know. And I want you to know I love you, too. Like a woman loves a man. But there's something very special here that I want to keep."

"What?"

"You. You're young and beautiful and kissing is important to you. It doesn't mean that much to me anymore. Perhaps I've done too much of it. Don't you see? If we were to keep kissing, we would ruin what we have. We wouldn't be any different than anybody else. This way we're special."

"You mean we're never going to kiss again?"

"Yes, we're going to remain special forever."

"Oh."

Fanny laughed.

"What's so funny? You do love me, don't you, Miss Kemble?"

"Yes. I said I did and I meant it. Don't be upset. You've made me very happy."

"Then why are there tears in your eyes?"

"That's what comes from being special."

# V
# HANOVER

ROBERT AND FANNY WERE SPECIAL. This meant they couldn't kiss, but Robert could watch Fanny perform from a box seat, run errands for her during the intermission, and sit in her dressing room after the show. Being special didn't bother him; if anything, it put him more at ease. He didn't have to think of things to say, and he could listen to what Fanny had to say without being afraid to admit he didn't know every person, place, or thing she mentioned. In other words, he could be himself.

Fanny discovered being special meant constantly reassuring Robert of her affection for him—especially when he brought up the subject of her former husband Pierce Butler. Fanny had been through this particular drama of insecurity with men far more adept at hiding their fears than Robert, but there was a limit to how much she could take. One day, while picnicking on Capri, she decided not to give Robert the petty satisfaction he was continually looking for. She told him that Pierce Butler simply adored her. "It was just like you might read in a fairy tale or hear in a popular song. We married very quickly."

"Then the truth about him came out, right?"

"Yes, but not in the way you think. He was always very loving and considerate."

"Then why'd you leave him?"

"He was very insecure. He kept wanting me to assure him of my love."

"So you didn't really love him?"

"Pierce ended a long search for someone I *could* love. I've always had plenty of men in love with me; the problem was finding someone to love back. Someone I could live with in harmony. Someone who agreed with my tastes, beliefs, and values. Someone I could respect."

"And Pierce was all of those things?"

"More. The problem was he never did anything about them."

"Mother says they're the worst kind of people. They think they're not doing anything wrong, but they're just as guilty as the person who's being cruel. If you're not actively fighting evil, you're letting it spread."

"That's probably true, but I can also see Pierce's point. He wasn't so sure that interfering in other people's affairs was always a good thing. He used to say more damage is done in the name of what's good than anything else. Cruelty is easy once you believe you're doing the right thing."

Robert said it was the other way around. "Doing what's right is the hardest thing in the world. When I was at St. John's, I could've told everybody I was a Catholic, but I didn't. I told the truth. I spoke out against what I didn't believe in, and I took my punishment like a man. I may not have been very happy, but at least I can look back and know I did the right thing."

"Don't you think you could've maintained your integrity as a Unitarian without offending everybody in the school?"

"I didn't offend everybody in the school. They offended me. I just did what was right."

"But who determines what's right? I'm sure your religion teacher and the headmaster thought they were doing the right thing. Don't you see? When everybody's so sure about what's right, they don't take much time to consider other people's feelings. You might have enjoyed St. John's and still been a good Unitarian had you tried to *understand* your teacher's point of view. And they might've had a lot less trouble with you if they hadn't been so defensive. But you were both so certain the other was wrong, you felt justified in behaving any way you pleased. Knowing what's right isn't always what's best. It makes you strong in one sense, but it makes you less sensitive in another. That's what Pierce meant when he said doing the right thing is easy. As long as you're doing what you believe is right, you don't have to worry about whom you hurt. It absolves you from even the most terrible cruelty."

"But why should I consider other people's feelings when I know they're bad? Doesn't that only perpetuate the evil? How long do you think it would take the slaves to be free if the abolitionists worried about the feelings of the poor plantation owners?"

"How do you know all the slaves want to be free? How do you know there aren't slaves who have masters who take good care of them? Shouldn't they have a say in what the abolitionists think is good for them? Do they all have to be free because the abolitionists think it's right?"

"I can't believe there are slaves who don't want to be free."

"Well, there are, but that's not the point. Being sure about what's right and wrong often makes us think we can treat people any way we want and not feel bad about it."

"Is that why you left Pierce Butler? Did he do that?"

"Pierce believed as long as he did the right thing he wasn't responsible for how other people behaved."

"And you think that was right?"

"Of course not. But Pierce isn't the villain abolitionists have made him out to be, either. I thought I could explain that to you and you'd understand."

Robert didn't know what to say. He'd hoped to bring out a reason for Fanny to prefer him to Pierce Butler but found himself being asked to be sympathetic to him. If he did the right thing and held his ground as an abolitionist, Fanny would think he was insensitive. On the other hand, he couldn't sympathize with Pierce Butler without feeling like a hypocrite. Robert decided to do neither: "If Pierce was such a good person, why did you leave him?"

"For the same things we're talking about. He was so convinced his way was right, he never realized how horrible he was."

"But you said he never did anything."

"He let other people answer their own consciences. The result, or one of them, anyway, was that his slaves were always well fed and clothed, but many of them were horsewhipped by an overseer who thought *he* was doing the right thing."

"Why didn't *you* do something?"

"I told Pierce what was happening, but he said the overseer had to horsewhip the slaves when they didn't behave or he would lose their respect. In a way, he was right. After so many years of being treated like animals, they thought anyone who was kind to them was weak."

"So they had to be horsewhipped to keep them like animals?"

"Pierce said he'd love to tell the overseer not to whip the slaves, but his hands were tied by a system that was too old for one person to do anything about."

"Even animals respond better to kindness than cruelty."

"I know that, but Pierce didn't see himself as cruel. He thought running a plantation was like riding a horse. You always had to remind those underneath you who was in charge."

"So why'd you leave him?"

"I thought I could change him. My whole life in the theatre had been a struggle. Surely the man who loved me wouldn't be as difficult."

"How long did you try to convince him that doing the wrong things for the right reasons was wrong?"

"Fifteen years."

This sounded like an awfully long time to Robert. He was only a baby when Fanny and Pierce got married; when they met, he didn't even exist. "You waited fifteen years for Pierce Butler to do the right thing?"

"Yes."

"And when he refused to treat the slaves like human beings, you lost respect for him."

"Yes."

"So you think people should act when they feel a certain thing is the right thing to do."

"As long as they consider the feelings of others and accept the consequences."

"Oh, Fanny!" Robert cried and threw his arms around her. "I have to do what I know is right. I have to kiss you again. I know you'd lose respect for me if I didn't."

Fanny wrestled out of his grasp.

"What's the matter? We're special. You said so yourself. Lots of times. And no one has to know. But it must happen. We've got to stop doing the wrong things for the right reasons. Now!"

"Slow down."

"I don't want to slow down. And neither do you."

"Robert, please. There's something more important at stake here."

"What could be more important than our love? Or more right? I can't wait fifteen years for you to realize that. I won't."

It was the beginning of the end. The next day, when Robert tried to call on Fanny, she was out. When he went to the theatre, the stage manager wouldn't let him in. For a week, Fanny was always out or he couldn't get in. He didn't know what to do. He couldn't stop seeing her. Perhaps after they kissed that first time in Sorrento it might've been possible, but not now. Things had gone too far. Fanny had become the most important person in his whole life. But what had gone wrong? After what she'd said about Pierce Butler, he thought he'd done the right thing. He'd taken the responsibility of showing her his love. He never dreamed this would be the consequence. What would the rest of the summer be like without her? What would the rest of his life be like? He would go mad if he couldn't talk to her. He had to explain he was only doing the right thing for the both of them.

"I'm sorry, Miss Kemble is not in," said the maid several times a day for a week. Robert knew Fanny couldn't be out all the times he called; she just didn't want to see him any more. It was so obvious.

Yet he couldn't bear the thought of it.

Robert began waiting outside Fanny's villa. He'd catch her sooner or later. She'd have to talk with him or risk a scene.

"There's nothing to talk about," was one of the things Fanny said when she couldn't avoid Robert any longer. "Please don't display your emotions on the street, I don't hear well when people raise their voices," and, "Don't you think this kind of behavior is pointless?" were the others.

There was nothing left for Robert to do but go home. In the days that followed, he reviewed all that had happened and imagined conversations in which he told Fanny what he wanted her to hear. That she hadn't allowed that to happen frustrated him. He became angry with her for having done nothing to save their relationship.

Then came the letter from Heinrich. He was taking classes at a school in Hanover. He wanted Robert to join him. They could get rooms together overlooking the Leine.

Robert was on the next train to Hanover. The night he arrived, Heinrich took him to a performance of *Die Zauberflote*. Life was already looking better. In the year to come, they dined out frequently, became connoisseurs of Rhine wines, went to the opera, and attended every concert that listed a work by Mozart. Among Henrich's friends, Robert was known as the one whose heart had been broken by a famous American actress.

During the winter of 1854, the boys read Goethe, studied Spanish for a trip in the spring, and went to parties: American-pioneer parties, Roman Emperor parties, favorite-literary character parties, circus parties, and members-of-the-opposite sex parties. Parties in rooms, studios, houses, hotels, and nightclubs. A pajama party in Ricklingen; a pantaloon party in Misburg, even a national party where Robert wore a postman's hat, carried a crook, and called himself a German shepherd.

The cycle repeated itself in the spring; only this time Robert didn't enjoy himself. He'd grown tired of dressing up in ridiculous costumes, and his German shepherd joke wasn't funny the second time around. What he needed was something different, something that could hold his interest for more than an evening.

"Why don't you tell me what's the matter?" Heinrich asked after Robert claimed he wasn't up for tossing glass jars against the door of two people about to get married.

"Did you ever have the feeling that things couldn't go on forever?"

"All the time. That's why I go to parties. I want to live it up while I can."

"I know, but doesn't the repetition of the parties bother you?"

"The repetition is what's so good about them. Every season there's a literary-character party, a mask party, an opposite . . . "

"Yes, but it's always costume parties with the same kinds of people. Even the new people are the same as everyone else."

"You really are a bore this evening."

"I'm sorry, Heinrich. It's just that I want things to be different."

"That's why we go to parties."

Robert went to his room. Lying on his bed, he asked himself where people go when they run out of parties.

# VI
## CAMBRIDGE

ROBERT USED THE VOYAGE HOME TO WEIGH HIS PAST against his present and consider his future. How much time had he wasted? How much was left to him? What was the best way to spend it? How could he enjoy himself without becoming bored? Until the time he grew tired of his life in Hanover, only Fanny Kemble had been irrevocable. Everything else was there for him; all he had to do was want it. And all of it was new. Every day held something he hadn't seen or heard or done before. He could indulge his fancies and not have to worry about tomorrow: there were so many of them. If he made a mistake or hurt someone, he could always make it up. He could even break a promise to himself. It didn't matter when every day was a Sunday.

Time played on Robert in other ways, too. When he was a student at St. John's, he survived by telling himself that his stay was only temporary. It never occurred to him that he was living a life there. He always thought it would all be over in another few months. All he had to do was hang on until the next vacation.

He felt the same way about Neuchatel, Sorrento, and Hanover. Except for one difference: he was happy. There the feeling of being temporary had the opposite effect. He wanted to make the moments last as long as possible. He wanted to postpone being taken away from them. Every day, he wanted a new Mount Blanc, a different *Grotto Azzura*, or a more imaginative costume party. Somewhere along the line, however, he'd become bored. Someone or something had placed a worm in his apple.

Francis and Sarah thought Robert should go to Harvard. It would round off his education and, after a few years, there would be a place for him in the family business.

Robert said he'd rather sweep chimneys than be a businessman, but Harvard wasn't a bad idea. His cousin and childhood friend from Brook Farm, Harry Russell, was there. So was one of the Lowell boys. Maybe he'd run into some of the old gang from Miss Peabody's. And maybe, if he was lucky, he'd find something to interest him. Keep him from being bored. Give his life some meaning.

Cambridge was a disappointment, however. It didn't compare with any place he'd been in Europe, and the college was worse. Shut off from the rest of the world by a tall brick wall. What were they trying to prove? Who were they trying to keep out? Surely not anyone who had seen the students. So provincial! And so smug! They all acted as if life outside of "The Yard" was a puzzle and they were the only ones who had the key. Did they have a lot to learn! And childish? Whoever heard of grown men wearing class ties and addressing the sophomores as "Mister"?

Harry Russell was there all right, but he was as excited about rolling cigarettes for the sophomores as everybody else. Didn't he realize how ridiculous he was? Probably not, considering the teachers. They made everyone else seem normal. There wasn't one who didn't look as if he'd been gathering dust on a shelf for a hundred years, and you couldn't ask them anything without being coughed at or spit on. Thank God he didn't have to eat with them.

And that was the good stuff. Several weeks into the first term, Harry pulled Robert out of bed to play football against the sophomores. "I've never played," Robert protested. "I don't even know the rules."

"Don't worry," Harry told him. "There aren't many." Nor were there any helmets, shoulder pads, or referees. Only the football and as many people as wanted to play. A Harvard tradition limited the number of players to seventy on a side, but the annual contest between the freshmen and the sophomores included every member of both years.

By the time Harry got Robert to the playing field, Professor Rawlinson was concluding his talk to the Class of 1860: "The failure of nations is the history of people not getting involved. Preoccupation with the self allowed the Hittites to invade Egypt and the Huns to conquer Rome. Conversely, ten thousand socially responsible Greeks were able to defeat over one hundred thousand self-indulgent Persians. Who do you want to be today: Hittites or Egyptians?"

"Hittites?" the freshmen shouted.

"Huns or Romans?"

"Huns!"

"Greeks or Persians?"

"Greeks!"

Robert had all he could do to keep from laughing. He didn't know who was funnier: Rawlinson for saying what he did or the students for taking him so seriously. "To some of you, this match may be only a game," he told the freshmen. "Don't deceive yourselves. The call to stand by your fellow man is a call to action. And calls to action don't come often. Today's game is a metaphor, an opportunity to be Hittites, Huns, and Greeks. To make history rather than just read about it. Who's going to be the first to carry the ball?"

Ordinarily, this would've been all Robert could take but, somewhere near the end of his speech, Rawlinson had caught Robert's eye. He penetrated the young man's cynicism and made him feel like the falsely superior people he'd been criticizing since the day he arrived. If Robert didn't accept the professor's challenge, he would be just as bad as them. Worse, he would be a coward. "I will," Robert started to say, but Casper Crowinshield beat him to it.

The students cheered Crowinshield and carried him off on their shoulders. Robert cheered too, but he wasn't as excited as he pretended. A chance to rise above the mediocre, to become immortal in the eyes of his classmates, had just passed him by.

Vowing to distinguish himself in other ways, Robert won an election to determine the Social Chairman of the Anonyma Society, played in several string ensembles with the Pierian Sodality, took part in a Hasty Pudding drama, sat coxswain for the crew team, and came in with the lowest academic ranking in his class.

And Robert's second year wasn't much different. With one exception. He learned something about his parents that was so disturbing, he felt they'd betrayed him. Not just once, but their whole lives.

The shock came in James Russell Lowell's class. Robert knew the famous poet from Brook Farm but had signed up for his course because of Lowell's reputation for easy grades and going off on tangents in the classroom.

This time it was the Dred Scott case. Robert didn't know much about it because he'd stopped reading the newspapers after his mother began filling his mailbox with depressing slave stories. Nevertheless, he was able to tie together enough strands of the discussion to learn that Dred Scott was a slave who once lived with his master in the free territory of Wisconsin. When the master and slave returned to Missouri, the master sold Scott to someone else. Then some abolitionists came along and told the slave he was free because he'd once lived in a free territory. The case went all the way to the Supreme Court. If Scott won, other slaves who'd spent time in a free territory could also sue their masters.

Scott lost. The Court ruled that if Scott had considered himself a free man, he never would've returned to Missouri.

Lowell, a staunch abolitionist, was outraged at the Court's decision. The way he saw it Scott never would've returned to Missouri if he'd known he was free.

"But you told us ignorance of the law is no excuse for committing a crime," one student objected. "Why should Scott's ignorance be an excuse for his having returned to Missouri?"

"Because Scott didn't commit a crime," another student answered. "His master did. His master had a slave in a free territory."

"But his master's crime, if it was one, isn't relevant to this case. Wisconsin hasn't brought him to trial. Scott has."

"That's like saying the man who pulled the trigger isn't guilty for murder because it was the gun that killed the victim," challenged a student who hadn't spoken. "The master's crime is relevant because Scott never would've had a complaint had he not been held a slave in a free territory. Whether Wisconsin chooses to prosecute the master is irrelevant."

"As more and more people contributed to the discussion, Lowell channeled the students' arguments into determining what rights Scott had as a human being and what rights his master had as a property owner. One student wanted to know why Scott couldn't have been freed by the Court and his master compensated. That led to an argument between those who held Scott was already free and those who believed the Court had acted responsibly. "Had the Court ruled the way you suggest," a student advocating property rights shouted, "every slave who ever set foot in free territory could leave his plantation. Is that fair to the owners who paid good money for those slaves?"

"How can you talk about fair?" challenged an abolitionist. "Millions of people have been reduced to articles of property. For such a government—and those who support it—I can have no feelings but contempt, loathing, and unutterable abhorrence."

Lowell told Saltonstall to stick to the issue.

"That's right," said the student who favored the Court.

Lowell let the remark pass. He wanted to give the class an opportunity to hear from someone closely connected with the case. "As an original member of the New England Anti-Slavery Society," he told the students, "I've had the privilege of working with the Shaw family for many years. Francis and Sarah Shaw's agents were the first to contact Dred Scott and the legal fund they established enabled him to sue his master. What does this setback mean to them, Robert?"

Robert was stunned. Secret agents? Legal fund? Dred Scott? "It was a severe blow" and "My parents were very disappointed" were the best responses he could manage.

Robert's best wasn't good enough for Lowell, however. "How will this case affect your family's men in Kansas?"

"Badly."

Lowell dismissed the class and Robert slinked off to his room. Why hadn't his parents told him? Even if he hadn't shown much interest in their crusade, they still should have said something. He demanded an explanation.

"You simply didn't care," Sarah answered in a letter. "You were having too good a time in Switzerland, Italy, and Germany.

But that doesn't mean we didn't try. How many hundreds of newspaper clippings about conditions in the South did we send you without ever receiving so much as a thank you? For two years we bought you a subscription to *The National Era* and all we ever heard was how boring it was to see *Uncle Tom's Cabin* serialized in 1852 after it had already been run in 1851. Even your reaction in Professor Lowell's class is concerned more with your own embarrassment than Dred Scott's fate or the abolitionists' defeat."

Nevertheless, Sarah apologized for the embarrassment she and Francis caused and promised to tell him anything he wanted to know the next time he was in Staten Island. Francis added a postscript: "We'd welcome whatever help you could give us, Robert. No movement ever needed help more."

Robert accepted Sarah's apology as well as Francis' offer to include him in their work. If he hadn't, they would continue to see him as the selfish person he already knew he was. But that wasn't Robert's only reason. The abolition movement might hold his interest for a summer. There had to be some satisfaction in it for so many people to have become so deeply involved.

That summer Robert learned of his parents giving Mrs. Chaffie the money she needed to buy Dred Scott and free him so he could sue his former master—slaves couldn't sue because they weren't citizens. He also learned of Francis and Sarah's paying off all the lawyers involved in the case. Except for the judges, the whole trial had been rigged. Even the cross examinations had been rehearsed.

The abolitionists' showcase failed, however, and so did Robert's interest in the crusade. Working out of the family home in Staten Island, he never so much as saw a secret agent or a gunrunner. Just piles and piles of letters—all of which had to be decoded or deciphered—and bank drafts—all of which were mailed to middlemen who cashed them, took their cuts, and passed on what was left to people in the field. Every once in a while, Robert attended a secret meeting, but all the abolitionists ever did was argue over whom they were supporting in the next election, what politicians had been contacted for contributions, which articles appearing in *the Liberator* should be reprinted in *The Christian Recorder*, how much more money was going to be spent on floundering projects, what speakers hadn't been heard in what parts of the country, how many more stations the Underground Railroad could carry in light of the recent crackdown in Ohio, to what extent John Brown's activities were damaging their image among moderates, and when, if ever, was the best time for an armed rebellion of the slaves. Robert had all he could do to stay awake. He couldn't wait to get back to Cambridge.

But Harvard bored Robert more than ever. Two weeks into his third year, he asked Harry to ask his father to offer him a job in the family's New York office. One month later, Robert was out of Harvard, out of the abolition movement, and into the China trade.

# VII
## NEW YORK

THEATRE, RESTAURANTS, OPERA, CONCERTS, AND GALLERIES. New York had them all and all in one place: Manhattan. The *real* hub.

Robert rented a floor-through near Battery Park. Close enough to walk to work but far enough away from Staten Island to have a life of his own, his living room looked out on a vista of steamers, schooners, sloops, and skiffs. Everything was perfect now. Except the time: there wasn't enough of it. And the job: he hated it.

"There's no greater bondage than being chained to a desk," Robert wrote Heinrich during the summer of 1859. "I work ten hours a day, six days a week. By Sunday I'm exhausted, but I can't rest. I have to squeeze into my one day off the six days of living that I put into my job. If I'm lucky, I'll be sent with a ship to China in two or three years."

A weekend with the Forbes family on Naushon Island was the closest he ever got. Four months it took him to get a Saturday off, and then it rained the whole time he was there. On the train back to New York, Robert decided what he really wanted to do with his life: head west. Follow in the footsteps of the famous explorer John Charles Fremont. Help settle the California territory. Maybe buy a ranch somewhere.

Robert asked his parents to stake him, but they had troubles of their own. Shaken by a crash in 1857 as well as the expense of the

Dred Scott case, Francis and Sarah had to choose between selling their home or cutting back on the money they donated to *The Liberator*, the Underground Railroad, and John Brown's army.

They sold the house.

In October, Brown captured the arsenal at Harper's Ferry. The raid surprised everybody, including the slaves Brown expected to join him. Hopelessly outnumbered, he surrendered. Some of the rifles used in the raid were traced to the Shaws; once again Francis and Sarah found themselves in exile.

Robert didn't mind taking care of the new house in Elliotville. With his older sister married and his three younger sisters away at school, he had the whole place to himself. He also enjoyed reading the newspaper on the ferry that ran between Staten Island and Manhattan.

The big news in 1859 was the upcoming presidential campaign, and everybody at work was talking about the issues that separated the candidates. Because he didn't want to be left out, Robert began reading more than the entertainment listing. What started as a way to participate in conversation, however, soon developed into a genuine interest. He even went to a few rallies and a debate.

The debate featured William Henry Seward, a Republican, and William Lowndes Yancy, a Southern Democrat. Seward, in an effort to win the sympathy of moderate abolitionists, claimed he wanted to keep slavery from spreading to the new territories. If it was up to him he would abolish slavery, but who would compensate the owners?

Yancy claimed the South wouldn't be able to meet the North's demand for more cotton if slavery was restricted. That would mean fewer jobs in the textile mills and higher prices in the stores. "Slavery," he said, "is as necessary to your prosperity as it is to ours. Granted it isn't a pleasant institution, but it doesn't harm you. We keep our niggers where they belong. The bad ones don't steal from you, the lazy ones don't keep you awake at night with their howling and prowling, and the few that can manage an honest day's work don't trouble you with their peculiar stench, which is very good in the nose of a Southerner but intolerable in the nose of a Northerner."

Robert enjoyed Yancy's rhetorical flair, but his mind had been made up from what he'd read in the newspapers. He was voting for Seward. But then Seward dropped out of the race in favor of Abraham Lincoln and Yancy gave way to Stephen Douglas.

Francis and Sarah hated them both. "Douglas pledges to preserve slavery," Francis wote Robert from Havana. "That eliminates him. Lincoln only opposes the expansion of slavery. Neither proposes to take action against slavery where it already exists, and both have repeatedly said they're against equal rights for free Blacks. The only logical choice is Gerrit Smith."

Robert had no defense for Lincoln's stand against equal rights, but he thought limiting the expansion of slavery was a step in the right direction.

"Nonsense," Francis replied. "Lincoln pretends to be on everyone's side so he can get elected. He tells abolitionists he will prevent the expansion of slavery, but he tells plantation owners he will do everything in his power to preserve it. You say Lincoln is morally opposed to slavery, yet he won't do anything to abolish it. What kind of morality is that? Lincoln only goes against slavery so far as it gains him votes. When he says he cannot go as fast as the abolitionists want, what he's really saying is he can't afford to do what he knows is right."

"What he's saying," Robert wrote back, "is he can't be as radical as you and mother would like. He has to consider other people's feelings. He wants to take his time, to work gradually so as not to force the South into secession."

Francis turned the argument over to Sarah. "The 'Declaration of Independence' states that any government which undermines man's inalienable rights should be destroyed and a new one formed. That's why your father and I are supporting Gerrit Smith. He'll kick the South out of the Union, if he has to, and place an embargo on her until she agrees to free the slaves."

Robert pointed out that an embargo would only lead to war. "And how many Northerners do you think would be willing to die for the slaves' freedom? I know I'm not. Fortunately, Gerrit Smith can't buy a vote outside of New England. But that's not the point. Every vote for Smith is a vote taken away from Lincoln, and every vote taken away from Lincoln helps Douglas. Smith can't beat either Lincoln or Douglas, but those who support him may determine our next president."

"You're the one who's missed the point," Sarah wrote back. "Do you think Lincoln really cares about the slaves? He's as much pro-slavery in his avoidance of the issue as Douglas is in his support of it. The only reason he promises to keep slavery from spreading is because he needs abolition votes to win. The more votes we can pledge for Smith, the more concessions Lincoln will be willing to make for the slaves. Smith would happily throw all his votes in the Republican camp if Lincoln would carry his anti-slavery platform a little further. 'No More Slave States' is good, but 'No More Slaves' is better."

"So why not be satisfied with what's 'good' now in the hope of getting what's 'better' later? If Lincoln doesn't get elected, the most you can hope for is nothing."

Sarah wasn't convinced, but it didn't matter. Lincoln won, and the abolitionists had to content themselves with what Robert had called "a step in the right direction."

Several weeks after Lincoln's victory, South Carolina seceded. Other states quickly followed. Now the radicals had something to cheer about. They'd been wanting to kick the slaveholders out of the Union for twenty years. Who'd have guessed they'd leave of their own free will?

When Harper's Ferry became a part of the Confederate States of America, *all* the Shaws celebrated. Francis and Sarah could come home. "Alleluia!" Sarah cried as she stepped onto the pier in New York. "Without the aid of federal troops, the plantation owners won't be able to suppress the slaves' rebellion. Freedom is at hand."

Robert wondered how someone who knew so much about slaves could know so little about Blacks. "You don't expect people who have been oppressed all their lives to suddenly rise up and battle successfully against free men, do you?"

"Don't you think two hundred and fifty years of slavery is reason enough to fight?" Sarah countered. "Look what it's done to me, and I've never even seen a plantation."

"The Blacks had a chance to rebel when John Brown took the arsenal at Harper's Ferry. Where were they then? Now John Brown's dead and what's left of his army is in jail. And for what? The Blacks can run as far as Canada, but they can't fight in their own back yards."

"Suicide has many names," Sarah snapped back. "Fighting armed troops without weapons is one of them."

Francis tried to tell Robert about the courage it took to escape from a plantation, but Sarah cut him short. The Blacks would prove themselves when they got their chance, and she had an idea that'd help them get it. Now that the South had seceded, there'd be no more Fugitive Slave Law. Escaped Blacks didn't have to run to Canada. They could stay in the North and be trained to fight in a liberation army.

But Abraham Lincoln had no intention of abolishing the Fugitive Slave Law. He wanted to preserve the Union—even if he had to reverse any gains the abolitionists might have made to do it.

The radicals were furious. They could understand Lincoln's not wanting to go down in history as the president who broke up the Union, but the nation wasn't worth preserving if it could only be held together by oppression.

Robert sided with his parents on this one, but for a different reason. He believed the South should be granted its independence or taken back into the Union by force. "No good can come from patching up the affair. That will only last until the next election, and then we'll have to go through the whole thing all over again. Unless the question of slavery is settled once and for all, it will go on forever."

Secretary of War Edwin Stanton gave the same advice to Lincoln, but the president didn't want to be cast in the role of the aggressor. He believed the South should be given every opportunity to rejoin the Union before any blood was shed. Lincoln's proposal for a compromise, however, made Francis and Sarah wonder if it wasn't time for New England to secede. If the South returned to the Union, the president guaranteed to protect slavery where it already existed, prohibit interference in the slave trade, and expand slavery into all the territories south of the Mason-Dixon Line. Lincoln's plan also included a provision to ship all the country's free Blacks to Haiti.

The idea that the only good Black was a slave had been around for a long time, but Lincoln's proposal gave it new popularity. Originally conceived by whites who didn't believe the two races could live together as equals, the plan was later endorsed by Blacks who'd become embittered by their second-class status.

James Redpath was the movement's chief spokesman and organizer. A white, British-born journalist who'd covered the Haitian Revolution of 1859, he wrote glowing accounts of the island's beauty and the integrity of its president, Fabre Geffrard. Geffrard believed Haiti's future depended on his ability to develop its natural resources, and he approached Redpath with a plan to subsidize the immigration of American Blacks.

With $20,000 from Geffrard, Redpath opened an office in Boston shortly after Lincoln's election. He immediately began recruiting people to write articles, make speeches, and publish a newspaper about the future of Blacks in Haiti.

In *A Guide to Haiti*, Redpath describes the island as a paradise "where the Black and the man of color are undisputed lords, where neither laws, nor prejudice, nor historical memories press cruelly on persons of African descent; where the people whom America degrades and drives from her are rulers, judges, and generals as well as authors, artists, and legislators." The Haitian government, furthermore, was prepared to give fifteen dollars to every man, woman, and child who emigrated and sell them land at prices they could afford with long-term credits. The island's new citizens would also be exempt from military service.

Politicians rushed to jump on the Haiti bandwagon. Here was a solution that had something in it for everyone: the Blacks would be equal, the whites would be rid of them, Geffrard's government would be stabilized, the prosperity of Haiti would be ensured, and the new immigrants would have their chance to prove themselves.

Black supporters of the program also responded. William Wells Brown wrote that "the descendants of Africa will never be respected in America until they leave the cook shop, barber's chair, and the white-wash brush. In Haiti, we shall demonstrate the genius and capability of the Negro."

Redpath convinced Lincoln to make the colonization of Blacks a part of his administration's policy, but he also roused the concern of those who hadn't previously taken the issue seriously. Among these were Francis and Sarah Shaw. In publications throughout the Northeast, they pointed out that colonization only weakened the strength of Blacks in America by removing the able-bodied and making those who remained feel as if they were foreigners.

Many Blacks weren't convinced. George Lawrence accused the Shaws of failing to face reality. Their delusion that Black's lives could be improved in the United States was criminal. It only made the degradation worse. The best way to change the black man's condition was to leave it.

But Francis and Sarah had black support of their own. Along with people like Frederick Douglass, they maintained that Lincoln's colonization policy helped spread the doctrines of prejudice and hate. It assumed that the viewpoints of whites were invincible and that freedom and equality were impossible. To give in to these beliefs was to admit there was a natural and unconquerable repugnance between Blacks and whites. The Shaws and Douglass said what barriers did exist were artificial and would give way before interest and enlightenment. The hope of mankind was in brotherhood, not in people like James Redpath and Abraham Lincoln.

When Robert read his parents had accused the president of being pernicious and calculating, he replied with an editorial of his own: "Abraham Lincoln is a pure, honest, patriotic man. He does what he does for the good of the country."

The president thought so, too, and went ahead with his proposal. On April 12th, he got his answer: South Carolina fired on Fort Sumter.

# VIII
## BALTIMORE

War wasn't a ranch in California, but it had to be better than an accounting house in New York. Or so Robert thought. What a relief it was to get away from that desk! He hadn't felt this good since he left Harvard. And he knew why, too: he hadn't been himself. If he'd allowed Harvard to turn him into a scholar or his family to groom him for the China trade, he would've forgotten whom he was before he became a professor or businessman. He would've lost some part of the whole. That's why he was so unhappy in Cambridge and at his Uncle Henry's office. An important part of the man who made up Robert Gould Shaw was missing.

Now he felt together again. All the loose strands of his life had been gathered and tied into the single purpose of preserving the Union. If only Grandfather Sturgis were alive! He'd be so proud. Robert was doing the right thing. Marching off to war as a *whole* man instead of just a soldier.

As he stood in front of the recruiting station on Lafayette Place, however, Robert wondered if he'd ever fire a shot. The line of recruits went for blocks. Many were Black. Otis Robinson, a former guide for John Fremont, had camped out in Thompkins Market all night. And he wasn't alone. Over three hundred men carried bedrolls. Others, like the Hannibal Guards, were already in uniform. Or a uniform of sorts. Organized to patrol streets in Harlem where the city police were afraid to go, the guards believed they could help their people better by fighting in South Carolina.

Robert asked the man next to him where all the Blacks had come from. The New York Seventh only needed a hundred volunteers.

The man didn't know. "Maybe they're bored with doing nothing all the time."

"Maybe they like the idea of killing white people legally," said another. "They done got all the ones in Harlem."

"Maybe they're looking for a chance to show this country what they're made of," said the man behind Robert. "Maybe if they help restore the Union, the government will start treating them like human beings."

Several men turned around to see who'd been talking such nonsense, but the man acted as if he hadn't said anything out of the ordinary.

Robert wondered if the man hadn't been hired by Francis or Sarah to free the slaves on any plantations the regiment came across.

"Sorry, boys," shouted a sergeant from a window on top of Thompkins Market, "but Uncle Sam doesn't need any niggers in this war."

Otis Robinson told the sergeant he was mistaken. "Blacks have always fought for America. My grandfather fought in the War of 1812; the first patriot to die in the Revolution was Black."

"Just following orders, boys," replied the recruiter.

The Hannibal Guards refused to move. So did the Blacks who were first in line.

Soon a colonel appeared at the window. "What the sergeant says is true, boys. Federal law prohibits Blacks from serving in the state militias. Why don't you try the regular army?"

"We're from New York," shouted one of the Guards. "We want to fight with New Yorkers."

"I don't care if you're from the Fifth Avenue Hotel. Our orders are not to enlist any niggers. This is a white man's war."

Not all of the country's authorities were so polite. In Pittsburgh, a squad of Blacks rented a public hall to drill in the hope they'd be called to duty. The mayor disbanded them: "I can't protect you from the nigger-haters, and I ain't having no nigger blood making a mess of municipal property."

When Blacks in Cincinnati organized a company of Home Guards, the police demanded the key to their meeting place, took away their American flag, and told them, "You damn niggers keep outta this."

It didn't take long for other Blacks to get the message. Even the anti-slavery *New York Daily Tribune* wrote: "If there is one point of honor upon which President Lincoln will stick, and which this paper supports, it is the pledge not to interfere with slavery in the States. The purpose of the war is the restoration of the Union. It has nothing to do with Negroes."

Francis and Sarah wrote that the slaves' freedom could not be separated from a victory over the slave owners.

Robert tried to console his parents with the idea that a Union victory might hasten the end of slavery, but Sarah was adamant: "Congress has no more right to establish an army based on race than it can require all the soldiers to be Catholics or Republicans."

"But the war has nothing to do with the Blacks," Robert tried to explain. "That is not why we're fighting. This war is to preserve the Union."

"Dis-Union," Francis corrected. "What Lincoln is really doing is making the black people his enemy in order to make the slave-owners his friends."

"You see what happens when you elect a politician instead of a human being?" Sarah asked Robert. "I bet Haiti looks pretty good to a lot of Blacks right now."

Robert gave up trying to reason. His parents' focus on the war and the role they believed it held for Blacks was beyond logic.

Sarah interpreted Robert's silence as a sign that she was finally getting through to him. "If only Gerrit Smith had been elected!" she lamented.

That was the last straw. "You talk about the Blacks being persecuted in the South and rejected in the North," Robert lashed out, "but did you ever stop to think what would happen if President Lincoln allowed them to enlist? For one thing, the whites would quit. The lower classes—the ones who will do most of the fighting—hate the Blacks for threatening their jobs. But you're so busy trying to free the slaves, you never think about the poor whites in this country. They're the ones who are fighting to preserve the Union. And what about the Confederates? How would they react if their slaves were going to be taken away from them? They'd never surrender. So which is better: to arm the Blacks and lose the Union or keep the Blacks out of the war and save lives—Black as well as white."

Francis pointed out that keeping the Blacks out of the war would only prolong the fighting. "The ones in the North won't be fighting with you, and the ones in the South will be working against you."

Robert voiced the popular opinion: "The South isn't going to last more than a few months. The North has more men, more guns, and more money."

Many Blacks weren't so sure. And if the North lost, it wouldn't be the whites who'd be enslaved. Hundreds of black families arranged their passage to Haiti; others tried to protect what few rights they had by working as cooks or laborers in the Union army.

Four days after Robert was issued a uniform, the New York Seventh was ordered to Washington. Meeting inside the armory on Lafayette Place, the soldiers said goodbye to their friends and relatives. Mothers brought snacks for their sons, wives pressed daguerreotypes into the hands of their husbands, and lovers exchanged tri-colored ribbons to wear on their wrists until they were reunited. Sarah gave Robert a small bouquet of silk flowers that had written on the stem "May freedom bring you back to me." Francis gave him a small derringer.

Even though the Seventh was only going to Washington until trained troops from more distant states could arrive, the city prepared a huge send-off. Stores closed, flags hung from buildings, and the mayor hired a company of Zouaves to lead the parade.

Thousands cheered as the doors to the armory opened. When the soldiers walked into the bright afternoon sun, confetti filled the air. Robert had never seen so many people. Over a million clogged the streets, filled the windows, straddled the lampposts, and lined the rooftops.

Two hours later, as the Seventh turned off Broadway onto

Cortland Street, hundreds of streamers formed a canopy over the soldiers' heads. What had once been a regiment quickly deteriorated into a blue wave bulging and surging its way through an ocean of people.

The first soldiers to board the ferry ran to the stern to watch the rest of the regiment. Others filled the bow and top decks to see the tugboats, steamers, and schooners waiting to escort the ferry across the Hudson.

But New Jersey was not to be outdone. Women came to the pier with cakes and cordials, while men handed out cigars and flasks of whiskey. Some of the older ones wore uniforms from the War of 1812. "Shoot a Reb for me," they told the soldiers.

The regiment boarded a train for Philadelphia, and Robert grabbed the first empty seat he could find. The man sitting next to him introduced himself as Eli Carlton. He said he was from Baltimore, but he'd enlisted in New York. "The regiments are forming faster here," he explained. "I don't want the war to end before I do my part."

Robert recognized Carlton as the man who'd said the Blacks were fighting so the government would treat them as human beings and offered him a cigar.

Eli reciprocated with a flask of whiskey. Two hours later, they were swearing the moon had three circles around it: red, white, and blue. "Our flag is flying in the sky," they told the other soldiers.

By dawn and Philadelphia, their eyes had the same circles, but the people who'd made their way to the Broad Street Depot wouldn't let them sleep. They'd piled enough bread on the platform to feed the entire regiment and cheered every time a soldier claimed a loaf with his bayonet.

Then the band began playing from the last car. The soldiers sang "John Brown's Body," "Yankee Doodle," and "Upi Dee." Robert felt as if he were at a picnic. Even the regimental song had as much play as fight in it:

We're the boys
That hearts destroys
With making love and fighting.
We take a fort

> The girls we court
> But most the last delight in.
> To fire a gun,
> Or raise some fun,
> To us is no endeavor.
> So let us hear
> One hearty cheer—
> The Seventh's lads forever.

This sharpened the men's appetites. They couldn't wait to sink their teeth into whatever food the people in Baltimore had prepared.

What they got was bricks, rocks, and pieces of iron. Anything that could be lifted was thrown through the windows of the train. Glass shattered in every direction, and those too stunned to dive for cover were knocked down by the flying debris.

Colonel Lefferts tried running the people's gauntlet, but they'd torn up the track. His only chance of escape was to stop the train, reverse its direction, and back out of the city before the track behind him was also destroyed.

The crowd had other plans, however. As the train came to a halt, women threw firebombs from their baby carriages while men used the smoke as a screen to storm the train, club the stunned soldiers, and seize whatever rifles they could lay their hands on.

Suddenly a shot rang out. Others followed and the rioters stampeded. Several died in their attempt to get behind something that would stop the soldiers' bullets.

Lefferts ordered his men to cease fire. Their war was with rebels, not civilians. If the people rushed the train again, the soldiers were to protect themselves with their bayonets. Under no circumstances was anyone to fire unless he gave the command.

But the mob knew it'd been beaten. There was nothing to do now but watch the train back out of Baltimore. Guns pointed at them from every window.

Except the first. That's where the musicians were.

Frustrated by their defeat and angered by the sight of dead friends, the rioters charged the unarmed musicians.

Soldiers in the car behind tried to help, but the connecting door had been jammed in the first attack. The few who jumped out of their windows were disarmed and clubbed to death almost as soon as they hit the ground. Robert wondered why Colonel Lefferts hadn't given the order to fire. What could he possibly be thinking of?

Nothing. From Lefferts' car, the rioters looked as if they were still running away.

Then came the flash of white light.

Robert didn't know how long he'd been out but, when he put his hand to the back of his head, it came back covered with blood. His derringer was gone, too. And so was Eli. A man who'd broken through the roof of the train was calling for dynamite. He wanted to blow the Yankees back to New York.

Robert panicked. Jumping from the nearest window, he saw the bandleader lying over a railing. Iron poles ran out of his back, but he was still alive. So many people were so busy trying to pull his uniform off, they didn't notice Robert. Up the street, into a narrow court, through an open door, and he was safe. At least for the moment. From a window on the second floor, Robert could see some of the rioters. They had a soldier cornered in a nearby alley and would've rushed him if the man wasn't holding a derringer.

The man was Eli.

"That ain't no soldier," someone shouted from the crowd. "That's Beullah's nigger boy."

"Welcome home, son," shouted another.

Eli threatened to shoot the first person to take a step toward him.

That made the crowd think a bit. No nigger was worth dying for.

Then, just when he had them wondering what to do next, Eli did a strange thing. He put his pistol on the ground, snapped to attention, and saluted.

# IX
## WASHINGTON

ROBERT CAUGHT UP WITH THE SEVENTH AT HAVRE DE GRACE. Fourteen soldiers had been killed, thirty-six were wounded, and nine had yet to report. Robert accounted for himself and Eli Carlton. He said nothing about Eli being Black, though. Nor did he say anything about standing by while the mob stripped him of his clothes and hanged him from a tree. With one gesture, Eli had refuted many of the assumptions Robert held about Blacks. Obviously, they could do more than run. And what Eli had done took more courage than fighting. His salute immediately placed him above the white people's violence, savagery, and cowardice. Eli Carlton was easily the bravest man in the regiment.

Colonel Lefferts announced that he would put Eli in for a commendation, but that wasn't good enough for the soldiers. They wanted revenge.

Lefferts told them their orders were to reach Washington as soon as possible. The capital—which had always been more Southern than Northern in its sympathies—was vulnerable. During the time between Lincoln's election and his inauguration, the city had been torn by dissension and uncertainty. People were confused. They didn't know who stood where. Or even from day to day what side they were on.

Especially the government's officials. When the Southern

states began seceding shortly after Lincoln's election, President Buchanan did nothing. Most of the federal army's 16,000 men were fighting Indians in the West and their commander, Winfield Scott, had grown so fat he could no longer mount a horse. The Secretary of War, on the other hand, knew exactly what he was doing. Or so he thought. On the day South Carolina seceded, he ordered 115,000 muskets and rifles shipped to five Southern arsenals and requisitioned 124 heavy guns for several forts on the Gulf of Mexico. When Lincoln demanded to know why he'd taken this action, the secretary said if there was going to be a war, the Union would need supplies in the South. If he could get them there before the firing started, Northern soldiers wouldn't have to carry them down.

Regiments in the capital also seemed disoriented. Many officers from the South had resigned their commissions as soon as Lincoln was elected. Others refused to take an oath of allegiance to the Union. Some, like Captain Schaeffer of the National Rifles, prepared his men to defend Washington against the Yankees, while several Northern officers drilled along the Potomac to prevent an attack from Virginia.

The soldiers didn't know what to do. Unlike their officers, they weren't allowed to resign. They could only desert. No one knew who was loyal to the Union or who was protecting himself from a firing squad. Not wanting to take any chances, Lincoln issued a call for Northern troops to protect the capital.

The New York Seventh was one of the first regiments to respond, and Colonel Lefferts wanted to see his men make up for what'd happened in Baltimore. The captain of the steamer he requisitioned had other ideas, however. A Baltimorean to the core, he ran his ship aground a few miles north of Annapolis.

Lefferts ordered everything but the rifles thrown overboard. The steamer didn't quiver. He then had the soldiers try to rock the ship loose by running from one side of the deck to the other. That didn't work, either. The men were so tightly packed, there was no room for them to move more than a few yards in any direction. Lefferts then tried to get the soldiers on the starboard side to jump up while those on the port side came down. Impossible. No one side could stay in the air long enough. The *Maryland* wasn't going anywhere, and neither was the Seventh.

But the lifeboat was. To the U.S. Naval Academy.

The midshipmen tried to pull their training frigate, the *Constitution*, alongside the *Maryland*, but the water was too shallow. The soldiers had to be taken off in lifeboats. By the time the Seventh reached land, secessionists had torn up the railway lines between the Academy and Annapolis Junction, and the Maryland militia had taken up positions on the main road.

Lefferts didn't know what to do. The people in Baltimore had prevented the Seventh from going through their city, Captain Harwood had grounded the regiment long enough for rebels to destroy all the railway lines west of Annapolis, and now an army had blocked the road to Washington. What if the capital fell before the Seventh could get there?

While Lefferts fretted about the war, the soldiers forgot about it. They took baths, strolled about the campus, and, in the evening, listened to the Naval Academy's marching band. Assuming a sturdy, strong-blooded posture, Robert entertained the cadets with his war story and confirmed their romantic illusions of battle. He even tried to convince himself that brave men were always brave and heroes always talked like heroes. Perhaps his cheap little escape really was a glorious experience. He wasn't sure now. And what kept him in doubt was Eli's salute. No matter how much he tried to erase it by asserting his own manhood, Robert could not overcome the black man's gesture of human dignity.

But he would have a chance to equal it. The regiment had been ordered to follow the torn up railroad track to Annapolis Junction and bypass the Maryland militia in the night.

In the first hour, the regiment didn't cover two miles.

Then the men's imaginations took over. With each step they expected to see the flash of a Southern rifle.

The third hour was the worst. Dawn had removed the men's fear of an ambush and enabled them to walk next to, rather than over, the ties, but the sun soon proved to be on the same side as everyone else in Maryland. It sapped the soldiers' energy, drained their water supply, and reduced their already slow march to a stagger.

Nevertheless, Lefferts' plan worked. The soldiers arrived in Annapolis Junction with two hours before the first train was due— plenty of time to forage for a good breakfast.

Sixteen-year-old Patrick Callamore was hunting for bird when a handful of Yankee soldiers began shooting at him. "I'm killed," he shouted as he hit the ground.

Two of the soldiers ran to where the boy had fallen and fired their guns at him. Somehow they missed. When they left, Patrick dragged himself to a nearby farm.

Patrick's mother was just getting out of bed when she heard rifle shots. She looked out her window to see her neighbor lying in a pool of blood. A group of men in blue uniforms had run him through with their bayonets.

Michael Callamore loaded his gun, but Mae stopped him. "Old Silas is dead; there's nothing you can do now," she said. "Hide in the basement."

Michael said he had no intention of leaving his wife to face armed soldiers.

"Don't worry about me," she said. "They won't shoot a woman, and you're more important to me alive."

No sooner had Mae replaced the floorboards leading to the basement than there was a knock at the front door. The soldiers wanted to know where her husband was.

"In Baltimore. On business."

One of the soldiers said he knew her husband's business and stormed past Mae into the house. Another demanded her money.

Robert didn't like what he was seeing, but he didn't do anything about it. The men had been looking for a target ever since their humiliation in Baltimore. Now one wasn't enough. If Robert tried to stop them, he'd find himself in the same position as the old farmer.

The soldiers helped themselves to whatever they could carry from Mae's pantry and set fire to the house. "This is what happens to people who do business in Baltimore," the soldiers told Mae.

As soon as the Yankees were out of sight, Mae ran into the burning house and tore away the floorboards. Michael lay unconscious on the basement floor. With the help of a neighbor, she dragged him into the front yard, but it was too late. Michael had inhaled too much smoke.

That's when the neighbor told Mae he hadn't just been passing by. Her son Patrick was also dead.

The soldiers, meanwhile, were on the train to Washington and singing. All, that is, except Robert. He'd seen more bloodshed in the past twenty-four hours than he had in his whole life. Yet no one seemed to notice. Or even care. The people in Baltimore had nothing against him or Eli Carlton. That they were Yankees was reason enough to want to kill them and strip them of their uniforms. The same was true for the soldiers in his regiment. The old farmer and the woman had done nothing to them. They'd just happened to be the first defenseless people the soldiers came across. Someone you'd buy a drink for at any other time and place could now shoot you or hang you or burn down your house. Cruelty had become its own justification.

Robert tried to assure himself that he was doing the right thing, but preserving the Union suddenly didn't seem as important as the lives it would cost. He should've headed west when he wanted to, worked a ranch until his family bought him one of his own. Which was exactly what he was going to do if he survived his three-month enlistment. Be true to himself for a change. Remember who he was. Do what he *wanted* to do instead of what he *should* do.

The train pulled into Washington at high noon. President Lincoln—no longer afraid of becoming a prisoner in his own capital—led the Seventh down Pennsylvania Avenue.

But no cheers rained on this parade. Earthworks had been thrown up at strategic intersections and all the bridges were heavily guarded. Barricades protected the public buildings, howitzers guarded their entrances, and soldiers searched everyone who entered. The few people who dared to venture out all had some place to go. And quickly.

Lincoln was the only one to pay any attention to the regiment. He welcomed his saviors to Washington and swore them into the federal service for thirty days.

Robert was quartered in the House of Representatives. As he lay his knapsack and overcoat on the space of floor that'd been assigned to him, a soldier asked him if his name was Shaw. Robert said that it was. "What luck!" said the man. "My name is King. Rufus King. My father is a friend of your parents. He found out you and I were in the same company and suggested I get to know you. I understand you went to Harvard."

"Only for three years," Robert replied with an air of boredom. He hated these types who always wanted to reminisce about their college days.

"It must have seemed like a lifetime," said King. "I wanted to go to Harvard, but my father didn't think it seemly for the son of the president of Columbia. *Comprenez-vous?*"

"You didn't miss much."

"Don't I know it. The most unattractive people I know went to Harvard. I just wanted to get away from home. That's why I enlisted. What about you?"

Robert liked King but not well enough to trust him with anything other than wanting to do his part to save the Union.

"Of course," King told him. "Your name is synonymous with contribution."

Something in King's voice made Robert add that he also wanted to get out of the family business.

"What do you think of our trip through Baltimore?" King asked." I sort of thought Baltimore went through us. I can't imagine the Rebels being any tougher, can you?"

"I hope not."

"That's the spirit. I can see you've been a bit disillusioned by all that's happened."

"A bit. But that doesn't mean . . . "

"Of course not. Look, Shaw, we don't have to assemble again until tomorrow morning. Why don't you spend the afternoon with me? My father asked me to drop in on some friends of his. It'll all be about as much fun as those railway ties, but I'd appreciate the company and I'll take you to dinner afterwards at the Willard."

The soldiers' first stop was the War Department, and the first thing Secretary of State William Seward wanted to know was why Rufus and Robert weren't officers.

Rufus had no idea, but Seward interpreted his silence as embarrassment. "The president needs men who can lead," he told the soldier. "Why don't you let me find you a commission? You'll be out of those rags in less than a month."

"That would be grand," Rufus replied in a hollow tone.

"And what about you, Robert?" the secretary asked. "Would you like to help the president, too?"

More time in the army was the last thing Robert wanted, but Rufus had already said he'd serve and the Secretary of State of the United States of America was offering him a commission in the name of the president.

"I should be very proud to be an officer," Robert replied with only slightly more conviction in his voice than Rufus. Seward was delighted and, to show his appreciation, gave the soldiers a letter of introduction to the president. "That'll give you something to write home about."

Robert and Rufus rushed to the White House. The president was meeting with a black citizens committee, but they could hear what Lincoln was saying: "There are broad racial differences between Blacks and whites, and these differences cannot be overcome no matter how badly you or I may want it. No two races can live together as equals if one of the races is inferior. It's just not possible."

"That's just the kind of thinking that created the differences in the first place," a member of the committee countered. "The only way of eliminating the differences now is to recognize all the people in the country as equal. At least in the eyes of the law."

"Look," said Lincoln. "Your race suffers for living here and we suffer by your being here and, harsh as it may sound, we don't want you remaining here. They physical differences between our races is a fact that cannot be overcome. That and not any way of thinking is the reason why it is better for both of us to be separated."

"But Mr. President . . . "

"Don't 'Mr. President' me. When you're ready to talk about a voluntary black colony in Haiti, I'll be ready to listen. Now, if you'll excuse me, I have some important matters that need my attention."

Robert expected the president to be in a bad mood after his meeting with the Blacks, but Lincoln seemed genuinely glad to receive the soldiers. He read their letter from Seward and said he appreciated "the inestimable service" the two had already done for the country.

Robert and Rufus were too excited to respond. Here they were in the president's office, and *he* was thanking *them*.

Lincoln then told the soldiers about the time he was an officer. It was during the Black Hawk Indian War. His company had been marching through a field and had come to a fence with a small gate. "I forgot the command for single file, so I had to order the men to dismiss and reassemble on the other side."

Robert and Rufus laughed too hard at this, realized what they were doing, and stopped. The office then grew heavy with silence. Robert tried to think of something to say, but Lincoln looked as if he was ready to end their visit. "We heard you arguing with the Blacks," Rufus suddenly blurted out.

Lincoln's face flushed.

So did Robert's.

"Are you Shaw?" the president asked Rufus.

"No, I'm King."

"I would've guessed Shaw."

Robert tried to distance himself from his parents by saying he thought everything Lincoln did was for the good of the country, but Lincoln wasn't listening. He was talking: "Personally, I wish all men everywhere could be free, but I'm not about to do anything which will jeopardize the Union. If keeping the Blacks in slavery will save the Union, I will keep them in chains. If freeing the Blacks will save the Union, I will break the chains. If keeping some slaves and sending the rest to Haiti will save the Union, I will do that, too. I will do less whenever I believe I'm hurting the Union, and I will do more whenever I believe I'm helping the Union. I will correct errors where I find them, and I will adopt new ideas so fast everything I do will appear to be true. Gentlemen, good afternoon."

# X
# Harper's Ferry

Sarah and Francis were outraged. Lincoln's speech to the black committee had demonstrated all the inconsistencies of logic, pride of race, and contempt for the oppressed as those of a colonizer. Which was exactly what Lincoln was. Or at least wanted to be.

Compiling the president's remarks into an article, Sarah accused Lincoln of giving racists permission to commit violence.

Robert felt like crawling under a rock. He'd repeated what Lincoln said to show his parents how determined the president was to save the Union, not for it to be taken out of context and turned into something that furthered their own cause. He had a good mind to resign his new officer's commission. That would teach his parents a lesson.

But no matter how narrow his parents' vision of what the North should be fighting for, Robert couldn't bring himself to resign. He had yet to fire a shot in his country's defense. To resign now would only make him seem foolish or insincere. So he asked for an assignment in Massachusetts rather than New York. That way he could fulfill his obligation to the Union and have as little as possible to do with his parents. He also knew that the Massachusetts Second would train where Brook Farm once stood. Maybe the site of his happiest days would bring him good luck.

They brought more. Robert's cousin and childhood friend, Harry Russell, had also joined the regiment. Pitching their tents near what was left of George Ripley's guest house, the two officers remembered visits by Emerson, Thoreau, and Lowell. Robert wondered if Emerson's hands were really as big as they seemed. Harry said they were bigger. "When you're little, everybody's hands look big. Emerson's still are."

Headquarters had been set up in the main house, but neither Robert nor Harry entered the building without recalling one of Hawthorne's ghostly readings or Charles A. Dana's German classes. Or wondering how something as perfect as Brook Farm could fail.

Robert thought it had to do with everybody going their own way. The farm was a good place to work for a while but, once the people became famous, there was no reason for them to stay.

Harry agreed but said there was more to it than success. He remembered Hawthorne once telling him that a man's soul could perish under a dung heap as well as under a pile of money.

On their free days, Robert and Harry walked through fields that once yielded crops, followed old secret trails, and picnicked in places where they used to start fires with quartz. It didn't seem like fourteen years had passed since George Ripley had shown Harry how to milk a cow or Robert took his first violin lesson from John Dwight. Harry said he still read *The Blithedale Romance*, and Robert told how he had become a hit at parties in Hanover by reciting "Der Erlkonig" in a falsetto voice.

"How could you possibly have remembered it?" Harry wanted to know.

"How could I forget it! I used to lay awake at night hoping the elf king wouldn't snatch me away."

"But the elf king only took children who went out at night when they should have been home in bed."

"You mean I did all that worrying for nothing?"

"As long as you were in bed, you were safe."

Seven weeks of training and nostalgia later, the Massachusetts Second broke camp with orders to attack Harper's Ferry. Robert couldn't believe his continued good luck. First Brook Farm, then Harry, and now the American Bastille.

Harry asked Robert if he thought what had happened to them

was more than just luck. "We may have been lucky to be commissioned in the same regiment, but to be quartered at Brook Farm and then assigned to a place that has as much importance in our lives as West Roxbury even though we've never been there? Doesn't that seem a little too lucky? Doesn't that seem more like fate?"

Robert didn't think so. "It was only natural for us to wind up in the same regiment. We're both the same age and we're both from Massachusetts. I'd call it good timing. And as for Brook Farm, it's a perfect place to drill. All the land's already been cleared and we're only nine miles from Boston."

"Then consider this," Harry replied. "The Massachusetts Second is the first regiment to drill at Brook Farm. It's also the last. Why? There's nothing wrong with Brook Farm. Not only that but if we hadn't broke camp a week late we would've missed our Class Day at Harvard."

"Coincidence."

"Is it coincidence that the people who influenced us the most were abolitionists? They taught us as much about the evil of slavery as they did about German, music, literature, or anything else. Miss Peabody could've written a book on the subject. And remember when Lowell had that discussion on the Dred Scott case? The summer after that you worked for the movement with your parents in Staten Island. Everything in our lives points to our returning to Brook Farm and our marching on Harper's Ferry."

"But I never cared about the slaves when we were at Brook Farm," Robert countered. "And I hated the summer I worked with my parents. The only reason I came back to Harvard that fall was to get away from them and the abolitionists."

"Then why did you ask for a commission in a Massachusetts regiment?"

"To get away from my parents *again*."

But Harry wasn't convinced. "You chose the Second because there's a force operating here that's bigger and stronger than both of us. Massachusetts was where everything started: you, me, the abolition movement, everything. Massachusetts was first to fight in 1775 and first to raise a regiment in 1861. And where are we going? To the state that brought the first slaves to this country. Isn't it obvious? Our destiny is inseparable from that of the Union. We shall rise or fall as the Union does."

"But the Union isn't going to fall."

"My point exactly. You and I are destined for some great thing, Robert, even if you aren't aware of it."

But the greatness Harry envisioned wasn't found at Harper's Ferry. The forty Confederates defending the town ran as soon as they heard an entire regiment was marching against them. Harper's Ferry fell without a shot being fired.

Fate or coincidence, Robert was given a lot of time to think about it. For the next four months, he and Harry watched detachment after detachment march through Harper's Ferry on their way to battles at Bull Run, Leesburg, and Ball's Bluff, while the Second's only order was to catch runaway slaves and return them to their masters.

Harry couldn't figure it out. Here he and Robert were at the vanguard of liberation, destined for greatness, and their primary function was to help the very people they were fighting against.

Finally, on October 22nd, the would-be heroes got their chance. Or almost got their chance. The Massachusetts Second raced through the night to rescue a brigade pinned down at Ball's Bluff, but they were too late. The ground looked as if it had been painted blue.

From Ball's Bluff, the regiment was sent to Seneca, Maryland. No sooner did they arrive in Seneca, however, than they had to return to Harper's Ferry. Once back in Harper's Ferry, they were ordered to Frederick. At Frederick, they were told to reoccupy Harper's Ferry. Finally, they settled for the winter at Charlestown, a wretched little place that'd made a name for itself by hanging John Brown.

Robert was assigned a room in the office of Andrew Hunter, the prosecuting attorney at Brown's trial, and the two officers wasted little time going through his files. Everyone from their parents to the Governor of Virginia had asked the court to grant clemency. The most interesting letters, however, had nothing to do with John Brown. They came from a Confederate spy in Worcester, Massachusetts.

These letters detailed the plot of Reverend Thomas Wentworth Higginson to raise money, kidnap Virginia's governor, and hold him in exchange for Brown and his men. Undaunted by the swiftness with which Brown was hanged, Higginson gave what he'd collected to James Montgomery. Montgomery, a former officer in Brown's army, planned to blow up the prison in Charlestown and free the remaining raiders. The spy hadn't signed any of his letters, but Robert sent them to Rev. Higginson anyway in the hope that someone would recognize the handwriting.

Then he went back to the files. With the people of Charlestown acting as damp as the weather, there was little else to do.

Except write letters. Most of what Harry wrote went to Robert's younger sister, Susie. The two had been friends since childhood and probably would've married had they not been cousins. Robert wrote to his parents and Heinrich, but he really wanted to write to someone like Susie. Someone whose letters would make him feel the way Susie's made Harry feel.

Harry suggested Susie's best friend, Annie Haggarty. Robert had known Annie since he was a freshman at Harvard, but he said writing to Annie wouldn't be any different than writing to his kid sister. On the other hand, he didn't have a whole lot of women to choose from. At least three in Charlestown had told him the only thing they hated more than niggers was Yankees.

On Harry's advice, Robert made up a story about a concert that reminded him of Annie. In her reply, Annie reminded Robert of a concert they'd attended with their families in Boston. Robert had forgotten, but it didn't matter. What mattered was that Annie hadn't forgotten. She told him he was the only man she'd ever known who could sit through a Mozart symphony and not lecture her afterwards about the quality of the music. To show him how much she'd grown since he last saw her, she enclosed a photograph.

Annie and Susie wrote to Robert and Harry through the entire winter but, by March, the soldiers were tired of letters. And of Charlestown. They wanted to move out. Engage the enemy. Bag some Rebels. Over a year had passed since they left Boston, and they still hadn't fired a shot.

Then came General Stonewall Jackson. The Confederate commander had a regiment under General Banks trapped in their winter quarters at Winchester.

The Second was ordered to the rescue.

Once again the regiment marched through a night of rain and, once again, they were disappointed. General Banks hadn't been attacked; he hadn't even seen a Rebel.

Once again, the Second began a long march back to where it came from. The spontaneous cheers and loud talk that had carried the soldiers through the night was now a grumble. It didn't seem as if they were ever going to fight.

That's when the first sounds reached them. Without waiting for an order, they raced back to Banks' camp but, once again, they were too late. Jackson's army had run through the camp leaving a wake of dying and wounded soldiers.

For the next two months, Banks' brigade—which now included the Massachusetts Second—tried to trap the elusive Jackson, but they had little success. When Banks attacked, Jackson ran. When Banks rested, Jackson attacked. While Banks recuperated, Jackson rested. And so on. By the time spring turned into summer, Banks' army was reduced to two-thirds of its original force. Now it was Jackson's turn. When Banks rested, Jackson attacked. When Banks withdrew, Jackson rested. Back through Strasburg, Middletown, and Kernstown—places that hadn't put up a fight the year before—the Yankees retreated. Time and again they were overrun by Jackson's lightning forces.

Banks sent for reinforcements, but there were none. All the Union lines were as hard pressed as his, and the newly formed regiments in the North had only begun training.

Abolitionists, meanwhile, clamored for the slaves' freedom. While they worked the plantations, their masters went to war. Recruits for the Union army, on the other hand, weren't so easily replaced.

Lincoln refused to listen. In his mind, freeing the slaves would only toughen Confederate resistance and alienate the border states. But he had to do something. The war was in its second year, and the North had yet to win a battle. Morale was low, recruitment was down, and the major campaigns of the summer were just ahead. If he didn't throw a wrench in the South's fighting machine soon, there wasn't going to be any war. Or any Union.

Finally, with the Confederates threatening to take Washington, Lincoln announced that the Union army no longer had to return runaway slaves. Because they were articles of property, they could be confiscated and used as animals or equipment.

The Northern army was doing more running than confiscating, however. General Banks had already been pushed back to Harper's Ferry, and he had no plans to stay.

Retreating past the school where John Brown had hidden the rifles smuggled to him by the Shaws, Robert saw a woman level a smoothbore at him. There was a loud bang, a puff of smoke, and a sharp blow to his side.

Robert saluted the woman. Whoever was watching would remember him the same way Robert remembered Eli Carlton. With courage and dignity.

Robert thought this a remarkably lucid response considering the fact that he was going to die. Then the woman fell and blood oozed from her head onto the porch. Robert could feel the woman's pain in his own head. Could she feel his pain where he had been hit? And did his pain keep shifting from one side of her chest to the other the way her pain kept shifting from side to side in his head? Wasn't this impossible? Who could be shooting him on the left side of his head, then running around to his right side and shooting him from there?

It was Harry. Only Harry wasn't shooting Robert, he was slapping him. First on one side of his face, then the other.

"I've been hit," Robert told his friend. "Save yourself. There's nothing you can do for me now."

Harry looked pale and angry at the same time. "You're not hit," he screamed at Robert. "There's no blood."

Robert pointed to a bullet hole in his coat.

Harry ripped open the jacket. A bullet was imbedded in Robert's pocket watch.

"I usually carry it in my fob," Robert explained, "but I put it in my vest because we were running."

"I'll cover for you first," Harry told Robert.

Robert broke for the nearest large tree. Rebel bullets whizzed about his head like so many retreating Yankees. A child stared at a woman lying in a pool of blood. Robert reached the tree, pulled out his revolver, and turned to cover Harry.

Only Harry wasn't there.

# XI
## ANTIETAM

THE SERIES OF UNION DEFEATS THAT BEGAN IN THE SPRING OF 1862 continued through the summer. On every front, numerically inferior Confederate forces outwitted and overran their Northern counterparts. Lincoln searched for ways to turn the tide but nothing worked. The Rebels knew the land, received help from the local people, and relied on their slaves to carry supplies, build fortifications, and work the plantations. Better fed and better rested, they could attack larger Union armies and then retreat to barricades that'd already been constructed for them. Northern soldiers, on the other hand, had to forage for food, build their own defenses, and expose themselves in unfamiliar territory.

Union generals knew there was little they could do about the land and the hostile people, but Lincoln had the power to hit the Rebels where it would hurt them the most: their slaves.

But Lincoln was adamant. The purpose of the war was to preserve the Union.

The Union generals pointed out that the purpose of the war was to win. Confederate armies under Robert E. Lee were crossing the Potomac into Western Maryland. If the president didn't free the slaves soon, there wouldn't be a Union to preserve.

Lincoln claimed freeing the slaves would destroy the Union

faster than anything else. It would eliminate the possibility of a compromise and encourage the Rebels to retaliate on the prisoners they took.

This quieted the generals in Washington, but those in the field became increasingly more frustrated. In their eyes, Lincoln was the best man on the Confederates' side. Some called him a traitor; others questioned his ability to organize anything more effective than a retreat. Robert's idol, John Charles Fremont, then took the war into his own hands. As Commander of the Western Department, he freed all the slaves in Missouri. Shortly afterwards, Lincoln freed Fremont of all his duties as a general.

Most of the soldiers, however, didn't think it mattered whether Lincoln freed the slaves. They knew that no slavery existed where there was a Union army, and no announcement from Washington was going to free any Blacks where there wasn't one. And as for putting the Confederates in a position from which there could be no compromise, few Yankees who ever lived through a Rebel attack believed a more desperate violence was possible.

Robert just didn't care. Ever since Harry's death, all he wanted was to go home. He never knew he could be so lonely. Having lightened each other's burden of cold floors, wet uniforms, hateful secessionists, and endless meals of hardtack, the two friends had become close to each other in ways that wouldn't have been possible in civilian life. It was almost as if, when Harry died, a large part of Robert had died, too. He tried to tell Annie how he felt, but she didn't understand. In Annie's world, she was still "special."

When Robert first enlisted in the New York Seventh, he was special, too. He'd been born into a good family and sent to the best schools. He could play the violin, sing in a choir, and speak several languages. There weren't many people who'd been given the same opportunities, or— so he thought—made as much of them.

This feeling of specialness increased when he first signed up to fight in the war. His family was proud of him and he was proud of himself. He'd spent hours admiring the way he looked in his stiff new private's uniform with the gray trim and, when he marched down Broadway with the Seventh, he kept turning his body to reflect the sun off his shiny gold buttons. He took pleasure in the cheers of more than a million onlookers. They confirmed his specialness.

But after the riot in Baltimore, Robert realized that he wasn't unique. The once proud uniform with the glorious buttons had made him a part of a whole from which his specialness could not be detected. Eli Carlton hadn't died because he was Eli Carlton. He died because he was an anonymous part of a whole that represented something horrible to the people of Baltimore. Robert was a part of that horribleness, too, though he didn't realize it at the time. When he jumped from the train, he was running to save his life, but the possibility of his actually dying never entered his head.

Harry's death changed all that. He'd been special, too. He had grown up on Brook Farm, went to Miss Peabody's School, attended Harvard, and worked for the abolition movement. He'd good reasons to believe he was destined for some greatness. Everything in the war pointed to it: he'd trained on the site of the commune, become close friends again with Robert, marched on Harper's Ferry, and slept in the courthouse where John Brown was tried. Yet, *Harry had died*. He wasn't special after all. And neither was Robert. Whether he lived or died had nothing to do with who he was or where he had been or what he knew.

When Robert shared these thoughts with Annie, she wrote that he *was* special. He was educated and refined. He could have stayed in his uncle's accounting house and grown rich, but he gave up his material comfort to preserve the Union. In her eyes, he was more than special: he was a hero. And so was Harry. His name was on everybody's lips, and his father had erected a memorial to him in the lobby of the office building. In a way, Harry was more alive now than when he was living.

Robert had to laugh at this notion. Harry was no hero. If anything, he was a fool for signing up for the opportunity to be killed. That's what all the fighting came down to in the end. This business of preserving the Union was pure poppycock. What did it matter if the Confederacy was independent? Whose lives would be seriously affected one way or the other? Robert had done the right thing when he left the family business, but he'd allowed the war to distract him from the person he really was. Enlisting was his first mistake; accepting a commission was his second. Now, after two years of frustration and death, all he could hope to do was protect himself from the mistakes of those who were running the war.

This was no easy task. At times, it was almost impossible. When Colonel Lefferts led the New York Seventh into Baltimore, Eli Carlton was alive. Twenty-four hours after Colonel Baker marched into Stonewall Jackson's trap at Ball's Bluff, Robert was writing James Russell Lowell that his nephew, Jim, was dead. Then General Banks repeated Baker's mistake, and the Second had been on the run ever since. Hundreds of soldiers, including his best friend, were dead. And why? Because of mistakes. Lefferts, Baker, and Banks all made mistakes, and Eli, Jim, and Harry paid for them.

But Harry had made a mistake of his own. He believed he was special. Destined for greatness, he never thought he'd get shot helping his cousin. Robert would never forgive him for that. Or himself for letting Harry die.

And from what Robert heard, the war was going to get worse before it got better. Lee was thirty miles outside of Washington, and rumor had it the British were coming in on the Confederates' side. For over a year now, Queen Victoria had been sending guns and ammunition to the Rebels who supplied the British mills with cotton. If she sent troops to protect her interests, the Union cause would be lost.

Freeing the slaves was the country's only hope for avoiding war with Britain. Parliament, which had outlawed slavery in 1833, could not support the Confederacy if secession were no longer the issue. And it really was slavery, after all, that caused the South to secede in the first place. They could call it "states rights" and Lincoln could talk about "preserving the Union," but the truth of the matter was slavery.

Lincoln finally admitted this and agreed to free the slaves, but he didn't want his announcement to be seen as a sign of desperation or taken lightly. He wanted a victory that was important enough to turn his announcement into a blow against the Confederacy and, at the same time, rekindle the flame of Union patriotism.

But could the North provide him with the victory he needed?

"Absolutely," answered General George B. McClellan, though he'd recently shipped his wife's silver to friends in New York. "We outnumber Lee's army almost three to one. Our firepower is twice as great as his. All we have to do is wait."

"Wait for what?" Lincoln asked his commander of the Potomac Army.

"For Lee to meet up with Jackson and march on Washington. The Rebels have to take the capital if they want foreign recognition of their government. All we have to do is dig in and hold them off. The Rebel army will be depleted, Washington will be saved, and Europe will mind her own business."

Lincoln wasn't so sure. He didn't have much confidence in McClellan. Although popular with his men and a capable organizer, the general had a reputation for being gun shy. Many were the times he had the opportunity to pull a resounding victory from the fire of battle but held back. Maybe that's why his soldiers loved him so much: they knew he was afraid to take risks. Dismissed for incompetence after the Union defeat at Second Bull Run, McClellan had been reappointed when Lincoln couldn't find anyone who was better. Like it or not, the country's future was in McClellan's hands.

The morning of September 15th found Robert writing to Annie near the banks of Antietam Creek. Jackson's forces hadn't attacked the Second since they took 11,000 prisoners at Harper's Ferry. Robert told Annie that Lincoln should form regiments for the specific purpose of being captured. Winter and prisoners were the only things that had stopped the Rebels. Robert owed his life more to Jackson's victories than anything General Banks had done. In fact, the Massachusetts Second had lost so many men, it had to be brought under General McClellan's command for protection.

But McClellan had just what he needed to deliver a crushing blow to the Rebels: Lee's map for the attack on Washington. Found wrapped around three cigars by a scout on South Mountain, Lee's plan was to attack from the north and reinforce his army with sympathetic Marylanders.

McClellan decided to stop him before he reached Sharpsburg but, as usual, the general spent more time organizing than marching. Not only did Lee beat McClellan to Sharpsburg, he joined forces with Jackson.

Nevertheless, the element of surprise was still McClellan's, and his first shells found their mark in a solid line of sleeping Confederates.

From his position above Antietam Creek, Robert could see grey bodies flying in every direction. The survivors raced toward a nearby cornfield as if they thought the tall stalks would protect them from the Union's heavy shells.

McClellan sent General Hooker's regiment into the cornfield and ordered his artillery to fire on any Rebels trying to escape from the far side.

Only the Rebels never came out.

General Mansfield's corps was next into the field, but they couldn't flush the Rebels out, either. As the fighting armies felled more and more cornstalks, McClellan saw why: the Confederates had been reinforced by a brigade that entered the field from an adjacent wood.

While Hooker and Mansfield tried to break the Confederates' resistance, the Massachusetts Second was moved to an orchard bounded on one side by a rail fence. Robert could hear the exchanges that took place in the cornfield, but he had no idea what was going on until he found himself on the flank of another Rebel counterattack. Yelling like madmen, the secessionists hurled themselves at Hooker's and Mansfield's armies.

Robert ordered his men to fire.

Hundreds of Southerners clutched the air and fell. The rest acted as if some kind of unfair trick had been played on them. Caught in the crossfire between the Second and the main column, the stunned Rebels withered.

Hooker and Mansfield now threw everything they had at the Confederates. Pockets of Rebels tried to regroup, but they were quickly scattered. Most of the others just wavered, broke, and ran for their lives. A few, however, showed no fear of the lead that flew at them. Even when they were completely surrounded, they continued to fight. One Rebel actually charged the entire Union army, killing one officer with his pistol and taking General Mansfield's life with his sword.

But Mansfield wasn't enough; the Rebel wanted Hooker, too. A score of bayonets and bullets confronted him, but he kept slashing away at anyone who stood in his way. Grabbing the rifle of a falling Yankee, he managed to fire a shot through the armpit of Hooker's coat before he could be stopped. Ninety-six bullets riddled the Rebel's body.

Hoping to keep the enemy running, McClellan ordered General Sumner to clear the cornfield of Confederates. Wave after wave of Union blue poured over what was once a farm but, Like Hooker and Mansfield before him, Sumner couldn't get through to the other side.

Had McClellan ordered his entire force against Lee and Jackson, he might've ended the war. His decision to send first Hooker, then Mansfield, and finally Sumner, however, enabled the Confederates to fight three armies one at a time. The result was a draw.

But a draw for the Union was as good as a win. Five days later, Lincoln announced that as of January 1st, 1863, all slaves in the rebellious states would be free. Forever!

# XII
## STATEN ISLAND

ANNIE HAGGARTY, LIKE ROBERT, WAS BORN INTO A LIFE OF WEALTH and comfort. Her parents, like the Shaws, believed they should make the world a better place for their daughter to live in. Instead of devoting their lives to worthy causes, however, the Haggartys protected Annie from society's evils by raising her on an isolated farm in the Berkshire Mountains. Their plan was to teach Annie the difference between right and wrong. Then, when she was old enough not to be curious about anything she didn't understand, she could be sent to a finishing school in Boston.

It was at the finishing school that Annie met Susie Shaw. They were the same age, but Susie seemed older. She had lived in New York and Europe. She spoke French, played the violin and the piano, wore white in the summer and blue in the winter, took a bath every day, and received messages from men who wanted to walk with her in the public garden. In fact, Susie spent so much time in the garden during her first term of finishing school, she came down with a tan. Not wanting to be mistaken for a farm girl, she began rejecting all but the most crucial invitations.

Annie was walking in the garden herself one morning—that and the common were the closest she could get to something green—when she saw Susie talking with a young man. "Annie, come here," Susie called. "I want you to meet my brother. He's just returned from Europe and is about to enter Harvard."

Robert said "Hello" to Annie and extended his hand in a way that indicated he wanted to shake hers.

Annie had learned in finishing school that gentlemen bowed before ladies, but she extended her hand anyway. To her surprise, he placed his fingers in her palm and, bowing before her, gently brushed the top of her hand with his lips. Something in French followed but Annie didn't hear it; she was too busy looking at Robert's smile. It blocked out the whole world and seemed to say to her alone, "I understand" and "Don't worry" and "You can do no wrong" all at the same time.

That was in 1856. She saw Robert several times after that but only when he came to visit his sister or she stayed with Susie at the Shaws' house on Staten Island. She never forgot his smile though, and he never forgot to bless her with it.

Robert and Heinrich had practiced that smile in a mirror for months. It didn't work on everybody but, when it did, Robert remembered to repeat it. He'd been smiling at Annie for three years when he ran into her and her parents at a Mozart concert. Afterwards, he entertained the Haggartys with stories of the prodigy's life.

Because she knew very little about Mozart or Europe or many of the other things Robert talked about, Annie mistook his showing off for intelligence. And yet, he never seemed to talk down to her. This was what made him different from the few other men she knew. He respected her in spite of their difference in age. He made her feel comfortable, less defensive, more herself. In short, every moment with him was just what his smile promised. He understood her, accepted her for the person she was, and assured her that he only remembered the precise impressions that she at her best, wanted him to have. The only problem was that the kindest, most considerate, most gentle man she had ever known didn't love her.

But the war changed that. It took Robert away from his home, his job, and the fast crowd Annie believed he ran around with. He became lonely. Harry and letters from his family helped, but they weren't enough to sustain him. He needed the concern and affection of a woman with whom he could share the feelings he couldn't express to Harry or anyone in his family.

Because she knew very little about why the North and South were fighting but genuinely cared for Robert, Annie proved to be a perfect correspondent and confident. Unlike Sarah Shaw, she never mentioned anything that had to do with the politics. Instead, she wrote about how *Robert* felt. When he was angry, she was angry; when he was sad, her sadness comforted him; when he was lonely, she showed him that he was missed. She became close to him and, after Harry died, she wrote to him every day.

Although Robert's letters were filled more with talk about himself than anything else, Annie found them romantic and exciting. And the places he wrote from—Winchester, Charlestown, Martinsburg—conjured images of him calling on her in his officer's uniform and their dancing through a plantation while dozens of southern belles looked on in envy.

Annie never told Robert about this fantasy. Instead, she tried to keep his spirits up by showing how much his letters meant to her. As their correspondence grew more intimate and revealing, however, Annie began to wonder why Robert never came home. Other soldiers did. As well as she knew him, he was still something of a mystery.

Robert explained how his responsibilities as an officer were greater than those of an ordinary soldier. He couldn't take leave whenever he felt like it. Especially now that the regiment was so hard pressed.

The truth was he was afraid. When Harry died, he promised himself he'd never get close to another person. The loss had been that painful. But he was already close to Annie. Too close. There was little danger of her being shot by a Rebel, of course, but he feared she might leave him once she found out he wasn't as wonderful as he'd made himself sound in his letters. If he went home and Annie discovered she couldn't love him, he would have to return to Virginia without his most important reason for living.

The inevitable day came, however, when Susie married Bob Minturn. With the battle of Antietam only hours behind him, Robert tried to distance himself from Annie. He reasoned that their whole relationship had been an accident of the war. Under any other circumstances, they never would have said what they did to each other.

But it didn't work. No matter how hard Robert tried to distract himself from their affection, he kept returning to it.

Annie had her apprehensions, too, and they didn't disappear the moment she laid eyes on Robert. He wasn't nearly as tall as she remembered. And since when had his skin become so tightly drawn around his face? These thoughts might have dissuaded another woman, but Annie refused to dwell on them. Susie's wedding had made her feel the need to shape her own future, and she decided to look through Robert's height and skin to the person underneath: the one who had written the letters. Until he proved otherwise, she would remain at his side, feel his presence, and reassure herself that she hadn't made a mistake.

She hadn't. And neither had Robert. In spite of their anxiety and his frail attempts to keep himself from her, their correspondence had produced a force in them that demanded each other's affection. They discovered they were as extraordinary in person as they were on paper.

This first became apparent at the wedding ceremony. Annie was one of Susie's bridesmaids, and Robert noticed how many young men found her attractive. The attention she received increased her value in his eyes. Especially when he saw that this favored person only had eyes for him. No other man could penetrate them. They were for him alone.

But the real test came at the reception. Robert and Annie were seated at a table that included his parents and one of the bridegroom's younger brothers. The papers had been filled with the news of Antietam, and everyone wanted to know what the fighting was like.

Under the admiring gaze of Annie, Robert told them. There wasn't a soldier who didn't walk away with some mark of the battle. He showed them the scratch a spent ball had made on his neck and told them about a piece of rail he'd brought home for his mother. It was only a foot long, but it had thirty-one bullet holes in it.

Sarah confirmed the number of holes and asked Robert to say something about the battle itself.

The officer dutifully recounted the events of the day—slightly embellishing his own contribution for Annie—and of the sad realization that thousands of young men would never have a chance to go to their sisters' weddings.

This cast a pall over the table, but Sarah used Robert's remarks to note that Lincoln could have saved many of those lives had he not waited so long to free the slaves.

Robert said the president was not responsible for every person who died in the war, but Sarah pretended not to hear him. Unless the freed slaves were now armed, she said, the war would continue for years.

Robert was used to hearing his mother go on about what she knew nothing about, but her snubbing him in front of Annie irritated him. He reminded Sarah that she had devoted her entire adult life to freeing the slaves; now that Lincoln had freed them, maybe it was time for her to give the country a break.

Sarah's jaw dropped. Francis blushed. Even Annie was shocked.

But no more than Robert. The words had escaped his mouth before he realized what he'd said. He couldn't believe he'd spoken to his mother that way. "I'm sorry," he told the people at the table. "I guess I'm just tired of all the fighting."

"I guess you are," Francis told him.

The groom's brother tried to smooth things over by pointing out that war affected people in strange ways. Made them say things they didn't mean. It could even turn people into animals if they weren't careful.

Robert wanted to say that the North's reason for fighting would prevent soldiers from deteriorating into animals, but Sarah cut him off. She told everybody at the table that the war hadn't changed her son and explained why he insulted her: it had to do with her wanting him to declare his Unitarian faith when he was a child.

Robert didn't say anything, but he was clearly embarrassed. He resented hearing that he'd always lacked the discipline to be quiet when silence was called for or the courage to speak when the occasion demanded. And the worst part of it was that everything his mother said was true. He'd been following the path of least resistance all his life.

Sensing how she'd made Robert feel in front of Annie and the others, Sarah tried to show her son she was still on his side. "At least he's fighting for what he believes in," she concluded. "He's not sitting on his hands and letting others do the fighting for them."

Now it was the groom's brother who was insulted. A pacifist who believed it didn't take much courage to hop on the bandwagon of war, he told the table: "The really brave man is the one who does what he thinks is right regardless of what everybody else is doing. When this war broke out, the easiest thing in the world was to enlist. Those who did were treated like heroes before they ever fired a shot. But there were a few men at the time who were brave enough to be called cowards. Defending your life or your family or protecting what's yours is one thing, but killing for the sake of saying South Carolina is in the United States rather than the Confederate States is only an excuse to commit murder. It's not the men who've stayed home who are cowards."

Robert didn't know what to say. He'd heard that pacifism had become a popular movement in the North, but he hadn't given it much thought. He'd expected to be admired and appreciated for his patriotism. Not embarrassed and ridiculed. It didn't make sense.

Sarah was also at a loss for words. She didn't believe the Union was worth preserving, but she'd cheered her son's participation because she thought the slaves would eventually be freed. It never occurred to her that Robert might kill somebody. Even though she'd been supporting violence for years, she never realized that people were actually dying.

Annie was the first to say something. Looking Robert straight in the eye, she asked, "Did you kill people?"

Robert said he was tired of talking about the war, but Annie wouldn't let him drop the subject. And neither would the pacifist. "Did you kill people?" he repeated. "Annie wants to know."

"When you're shot at," Robert explained, "all you can do—what you have to do—is defend yourself."

But that wasn't the answer the pacifist was looking for. "Did you kill anybody, Robert? Yes or No."

Robert took his pistol out of his holster. 'I'm going to take this gun," he told the pacifist, "and shoot you. Before I pull the trigger, you're going to jump on one of two bandwagons: you're either going to run for your life or you're going to defend it."

The man didn't move.

The soldier set the hammer for firing.

Beads of perspiration appeared on the pacifist's forehead.

The soldier started to squeeze the trigger. His pistol had no bullets in it, but Robert wanted to see just how far he could push his adversary.

A scream prevented him from finding out.

It was Susie. She saw what her brother was doing, and so did everyone else. They were looking at him as if he was crazy.

Robert slowly released the hammer, put his pistol back in its holster, and left the table.

Once outside the reception room, the full weight of his having drawn a pistol at his sister's wedding fell upon him. Antietam, Harry's death, his mother's insensitivity, and the impression he must have made on Annie rushed to the surface. He began heaving in desperate attempts to bring himself under control. Every sadness that ever happened to him rushed down the cheeks of his face. Not even the arms that came to console him could stop the flow of tears. "It's all right," he heard Annie say. "Everything's all right."

Robert started talking about Antietam and the Rebels that'd been caught in his regiment's crossfire. "It was a terrible sight. Our men had to be careful to avoid stepping on them. We didn't want them to die. After Sumner's charge, we ran out and tried to help. We gave them water from our canteens and disentangled their bodies. There were so many young boys and old men we didn't believe they could've possibly chosen to fight us. Some said they wished they'd never enlisted. One boy, who couldn't have been more than seventeen, said he just left North Carolina three weeks ago. His parents begged him not to fight. He wasn't a coward or a murderer. And neither am I. I'm only doing what I believe I should do, what's right to do."

Robert looked into Annie's eyes. She didn't say anything because she didn't have to. Her eyes said it for her. They told Robert he was understood, he was not to worry, and he could do no wrong.

# XIII
## STAFFORD COURTHOUSE

ROBERT KNEW NOW THAT ANNIE WAS THE ONLY PERSON IN HIS LIFE who really cared about him. In spite of what happened at the wedding, she still loved him. And her love made him feel special again. Not in the charmed way he once believed made people like him and Harry seem invincible, but in the sense that now he had a personal reason for living. One that went beyond politics and social issues. From now on, he couldn't let himself die. He had to keep himself alive for Annie. And anyone who tried to prevent their reunion was the enemy.

Including General McClellan. He could've routed the Confederates at Antietam but was happy to have kept them out of Washington. That meant that Lee and Jackson would have time to rebuild their armies. The war was sure to go at least another year.

But not with Robert. He'd paid his dues and earned a captaincy. What more could anyone expect of him? Now was the time to get out. Head west like he'd always said he would. And take Annie with him. He imagined them wearing western clothes and smoking peace pipes. Maybe they could do for the Indians what his forefathers had done for the Cantonese. Starting a ranch was a good idea, but a settlement with a trading post was better. That was money *and* freedom.

Robert wrote Annie about his plans and traveled to Lenox on

his twenty-fifth birthday to ask her parents for their daughter's hand. They were delighted to have Robert for a son-in-law, but Mrs. Haggarty didn't think it was a good idea to marry while Robert was still in the service. Wartime weddings were depressing.

Robert said he would resign as soon as he returned to Stafford Courthouse.

Francis and Sarah were less receptive to the idea of Robert's marrying than the Haggartys, and Robert couldn't bring himself to tell them about resigning his commission. That plus the wedding would've been too much of a shock.

Sarah claimed that a marriage would take Robert's mind off his work. "Why don't we just save any talk about weddings until the war is over."

But Robert wanted to talk now. He said that if he thought being married would make him neglect his duty, he never would have become engaged.

"You're engaged?" Francis asked. "Why didn't you tell us?"

Sarah didn't wait for an answer. "Do you know what happens to camp wives?" she asked her son.

Robert resisted asking his parents where they thought he'd been for the past two years. "I have no desire to take Annie to camp," he answered.

"That doesn't seem to be very considerate of Annie," Sarah countered. "How can you be a good soldier in Virginia and a good husband in New York?"

"Annie's lived without a good husband for over twenty years."

"Then one or two more won't matter."

"She's waited long enough. She wants to get married soon, and so do I. If you resist me on this, I will be very unhappy."

"How can you be happy knowing there are people in chains?"

It went on like this for over an hour.

Robert wrote Annie that his parents were thrilled about the wedding. His mother especially liked the idea of a ceremony at Christmas, but he wondered if it might be a better idea to wait until the spring. That would give him the time he needed to complete his duties rather than leave them for someone else. But if she wished him to, he was prepared to leave Virginia within twenty-four hours of receiving her next letter. His bags were already packed. All she had to do was say the word.

Annie had nothing against a spring wedding as long as it was someone else's. Christmas was her favorite time of year; that's why she'd chosen it. And she'd already told everybody she knew. To change the date now would make people think something was wrong. And if she allowed Robert to postpone the ceremony, who could say he wouldn't do it again? Already their relationship was suffering a crisis. How she handled it would determine any that followed. If she refused to change the date, he might see her as insensitive or selfish. That would do more harm than good. He might never marry her. The best way was to let him know how she thought without making him feel any pressure. Or rather, to get him to do what she wanted without making it seem like the pressure came from her.

Robert was amazed at Annie's reply. She really was the most extraordinary person he'd ever known. She admitted she would be disappointed if they couldn't get married when they'd planned—that showed she cared—but she also understood the position he was in. Whatever he thought was best would make her happy.

Annie couldn't believe it when she heard she was getting married in the spring, but she'd learned a valuable lesson: the next time there was a decision to be made, she would make it.

Sarah, of course, was delighted. The way Robert had been talking, she was afraid the wedding might've been sooner. Spring was a long way off; a lot could happen between then and now.

A lot did. On January 29th, Francis received a letter from Governor John Andrew of Massachusetts. President Lincoln, under pressure from the War Department and the failure of his "Emancipation Proclamation" to sabotage the Confederacy, had authorized the forming of two black regiments: one at Port Royal, South Carolina, the other in Boston. Andrew didn't know Captain Shaw personally, but based on his parents' reputation, he wanted him to command the Massachusetts 54th.

Tears welled in Sarah's eyes when her husband finished reading Andrew's letter. "I have not lived in vain," she told him.

"I'll write to Robert immediately."

"We can't trust our son's career and the future of the black race to the United States Post Office. You'll deliver the governor's letter in person."

Within an hour, Francis was out the door and Sarah was at her desk. On behalf of her son, she accepted the colonelcy.

Francis rode the overnight train to Washington, but he was too excited to sleep. He'd just finished his own letter to Governor Andrew, telling him how grateful he was for Robert's being given the opportunity to carry on his parents' life work. There was no question about his son's accepting the commission.

In Washington, Francis boarded the steamer that brought him down the Potomac to Aquia Landing. From there, he took a train to Stafford Courthouse and walked the last ten miles to the Second's winter camp. The road was rutted, water seeped into his boots and, as the sun fell, the temperature plummeted. But Francis never noticed. He was warmed by the same feeling that moved his wife to say she hadn't lived in vain.

Robert's first thought when he saw his father was that a Southern agent had killed Sarah or kidnapped Susie. Something too terrible to put in a letter.

Francis assured him that everyone was all right. He had brought good news.

When Robert heard, he almost wished something bad had happened. At least he would've been able to go home. Instead, he was being asked to see the war to its end. "It's a great honor," he said, "but I can't accept it."

Francis' face asked for an explanation.

Robert wanted to tell him the truth, but he knew his father wouldn't understand. He'd devoted his whole life to freeing the slaves. How could he know what it meant to be tired of causes and fighting? To want to marry, buy a ranch, and raise a family. "I just don't think I'm equal to the task," he said.

"Governor Andrew wouldn't have asked you if he didn't think you could do it. Your mother and I know you can."

Robert read Andrew's letter. "Listen to this," he said. "'I don't want just any officer. This regiment demands a leader who can attract the support, sympathy, and active cooperation of many influential people. They should recognize in him the strength and purpose of an entire movement.'"

"That's you!" Francis exclaimed. "You've been an abolitionist all your life. When the war broke out, you were the first to enlist. You stood among the bullets at Antietam and won a captaincy. Who could possibly be more qualified?"

"Someone with more confidence."

Francis paused. He knew how important self-assurance was. "Did your Uncle Henry ever tell you about the time he had to go to India and load a ship? He was so nervous he thought his father wouldn't let him come home once he saw what Henry had brought, but everything turned out fine. The same will be true for you."

"Commanding a regiment isn't anything like loading a ship, Father. If Uncle Henry had bought merchandise that didn't sell, the family would've found something else for him to do. If I fail, many people will die, and everything you and mother worked for will be ruined. I don't want that responsibility."

Francis admitted that commanding a regiment of untried soldiers was an enormous responsibility; it was only natural for Robert to be afraid. "But fear is no reason not to accept the governor's offer," he argued.

Robert recognized his mother's words in this statement. Even the tone of voice was hers. He decided to tell the truth. It was the only thing he could think of for which there was no argument. "I know you and mother are very proud of me, but everything I've accomplished has been a sham. The main reason I enlisted was to get out of the China trade, and I never would've accepted a commission in the Second if I hadn't been embarrassed into it by Secretary Seward."

This came as no big shock to Francis. He'd painfully followed for many years Robert's unwillingness to commit himself to something serious, but he thought his son had finally come into his own during the last year. With the exception of what'd happened at Susie's wedding, he and Sarah were very proud of him." You've already contributed greatly to the Union cause," he told Robert. "Now you can contribute to an entire race. The Blacks are finally being armed; Lincoln's war has been ennobled; men are no longer going to die for cotton but for freedom. Not to want to spearhead this movement doesn't make sense."

Robert asked his father to see the situation from his point of view. "My enlisting and accepting a commission was for the wrong reasons. Whatever my accomplishments, they're tainted by my own insincerity. To accept Governor Andrew's offer would only continue my charade. I've been humiliated long enough; I want out."

Francis said he understood, but the truth was he was too disappointed to listen. "Your mother and I are very proud of you, Robert. Just to have been considered for the colonelcy is a distinction that we will carry with us to our graves."

Four days later, Francis was back.

Only this time he was with Sarah.

"Had you accepted governor Andrew's letter," she told Robert, "it would've been the proudest moment of my life. I could've died knowing I had not lived in vain. Your refusal is the deepest disappointment anyone has ever handed me, and I want to tell you to your face that I have shed many bitter tears over it."

Robert withered with guilt. All his life he'd failed to honor his grandfather's last words and do what was right. If he betrayed his grandfather again, lived with lying to his father, and allowed his mother to die in vain, would he ever find peace in his marriage to Annie? Wouldn't his dishonesty, insensitivity, and irresponsibility taint his love and ultimately destroy it? For Annie as well as his family, wasn't it better to sacrifice his wishes one last time for the peace and happiness of all?

Robert recalled Annie's letter about changing the wedding date and compared it with the words his mother had traveled all the way from New York to tell him. He remembered the opening lines about how Annie would support any decision he ever made and the part where she described their last few minutes alone together. She had pressed her cheek against his chest and felt the vignette she'd given him for his birthday. He promised to keep it next to his heart forever.

Robert could feel the vignette now in his vest pocket. If he accepted the colonelcy, his mother could die in peace. If he didn't, his mother's life would be wasted, and he'd have to carry the guilt, shame, and regret around for the rest of his life.

Robert said he'd accept the colonelcy. All he asked was that his parents bless his marriage to Annie in the spring.

Francis wept at Robert's decision and Sarah, for the first time since Robert was a child, held her son close for a very long time.

"God rewards a hundred times those who do the right thing," she told him. "Your colonelcy is my reward. Now I can die in peace."

# XIV
## Readville

ROBERT MET GOVERNOR ANDREW AT THE STATE HOUSE IN BOSTON. Already there was trouble. The Confederacy had announced there would be no mercy shown to any prisoners from the black regiments: the wounded were to be shot, the officers hanged, and the rest sold into slavery.

Abolitionists pressed Lincoln to retaliate. For every Union soldier killed or enslaved, they wanted a Rebel prisoner hanged or sentenced to a lifetime of hard labor.

The president said he didn't want to increase tension between the two governments. The Confederacy's next step would be to forget about the rules of warfare altogether. That would endanger the lives of whites as well as Blacks. Nevertheless, he didn't want to lose the abolitionists' support. For the past few months, they'd been almost singlehandedly financing the war, and he needed their votes in the upcoming election.

Lincoln's solution was to create a policy that satisfied no one but gave everyone enough to feel as if they hadn't been ignored. Letting his authorization to organize the black regiments stand, he made sure they'd never be formed by insisting all the recruits be residents of the states in which the armies were being raised. If Blacks enlisted at the same rate as whites, neither South Carolina nor Massachusetts would supply more than half the number of recruits they needed.

This kept the Rebels from writing into law measures more severe than those they'd already announced, but now the Northern whites were upset. The president had done nothing to insure *their* superiority. Many officers resigned their commissions, and whole companies refused to fight next to any Blacks who were being treated equally.

Lincoln had predicted this would happen, but he wasn't one to tell his generals and the abolitionists "I told you so." Instead, he enacted legislation to keep the Blacks in what the white soldiers would think was their proper place. There would be no black officers. The new recruits would receive only half the hundred dollar enlistment bonus of their white counterparts, and it would be paid after the war was over rather than at the time they signed up. In addition, the Blacks would pay a monthly clothing allowance of three dollars instead of receiving one. And finally, there would be no duration of enlistment. The Blacks had to fight until they died or the war was over.

These measures quieted the grumblings of most of the white soldiers, but many civilians interpreted the two black regiments as a sign of things to come. If the government was willing to let Blacks in the army, it was only a matter of time before they overran the factories. Especially if the slaves were freed. How would the factory owners be able to resist all that cheap labor? They'd replace every white they could. They had no conscience where profit was concerned.

The immigrants rebelled first. They were already competing with the Blacks for the most menial jobs. If the ex-slaves got into the factories, the whites would be on the bottom forever. In protest, a group of Irish workers set fire to a tobacco factory in Brooklyn. Twenty-five black workers died.

This inspired an army of laborers to march into a black section of Detroit, destroy thirty-two houses, kill several women and children, and leave more than two hundred homeless. When news of what the workers had gotten away with appeared in the nation's newspapers, Blacks found themselves attacked on the streets of Boston and Philadelphia. Even the rural areas were unsafe. Blacks were seen hanging above greens in Portsmouth, Rochester, Wilkes Barre, and Oberlin.

Lincoln reacted by giving the Blacks another opportunity to escape. Through two New York businessmen, Paul Forbes and Charles Tuckerman, the president began a campaign to attract Blacks to cut lumber on Ile a Vache. Forbes and Tuckerman had leased the island from Haiti and agreed to supply the local government with thirty-five percent of the trees they cut down. For fifty dollars apiece, the businessmen promised to provide transportation, land, housing, work, and equal opportunity to every black man, woman, and child who emigrated.

Governor Andrew was undaunted. To combat Lincoln, the Confederates, the Union soldiers, the factory workers, and the colonizers, Andrew established what he called the Black Committee. Made up of one hundred wealthy abolitionists from every state in the Union, the committee would recruit Blacks, provide them with false proofs of residency, and smuggle them to the regiment's training camp in Readville.

In their enthusiasm for the project, however, the members of the Black Committee never questioned whether any black people wanted to enlist. All their recruiters returned with the same story: there was no reason for the Blacks to fight. At a meeting in Boston, Theodore Tilton told William Lloyd Garrison that when the war started and the whites believed it'd be over within a few weeks, black people weren't good enough but, now that some real fighting was taking place, the Blacks were expected to go out and get killed for the white man's Union.

Others protested that only a fool would fight for a government that proclaimed freedom for Blacks on one hand and refused to promote them on the other. "What kind of freedom is that?" Otis James wanted to know. "And look what happens to us if we're captured. We'll either be killed or sold into slavery. You call that opportunity?"

The abolitionists' first response was to try to shame the Blacks into volunteering. Garrison told the people assembled to hear him that they'd been crying for a chance to show what they could do for the Union. "Well, now you have that chance. Who's going to be the first to step forward and claim it?"

No one moved.

In Rochester, Frederick Douglass tried the same approach as Garrison: "To say you won't be soldiers because you can't be colonels is like saying you won't go in the water until you've learned to swim. To be allowed in the army at all is a great concession. If you can't have the whole loaf at once, can't you be satisfied with a slice in the meantime?"

Not one enlistment.

"Your country is offering you a musket," Wendell Phillips told the Blacks that'd gathered at Boston's Joy Street Church. "The question is: will you of Massachusetts take it? I hear some of you are afraid to be captured. Do you intend to be taken prisoner?"

"It's not cowardice," R. J. Simmons told Phillips. "It's self-respect. If Lincoln wants us to fight, give us the rights of citizens and soldiers. We'd tear the stomach out of this war in a week."

Robert, meanwhile, was discovering that idealistic whites were easier to recruit than realistic Blacks. Hundreds of abolitionists from the best families in the East applied. He interviewed Russells, Lowells, and Cabots, listened to the pleas of Putnams, Endicotts, and Saltonstalls, and tried to find places for Peabodys, Quincys, and Higginsons. One of the first to be accepted was William Simkins, a former student of Miss Peabody, a graduate of Harvard, and a friend of Harry Russell. Simkins' reasons for wanting to join the regiment set a standard by which all the other applicants were measured: "This is no easy decision," he told Robert. "It took a lot of hard thinking. But the result is obvious: the black regiment is an experiment whose time has come. And the sooner we do it the better. If we're successful, we'll shorten the war; if we fail, we'll discover the truth about these people and rid ourselves of a lot of false hopes."

In choosing his officers, Robert had a tremendous advantage over commanders in other regiments: he didn't have to take anyone in line for promotion. The staff he assembled was easily the most elite in the Union army. All were veterans with a least two years of college. The average age was twenty-three.

Robert's lieutenant colonel was Edward Hallowell. His younger brother was also in the regiment, and his older brother was the Black Committee's treasurer. The Hallowells' parents were known as the Shaws of Philadelphia.

Wilkie James, the oldest brother of William and Henry, was named the regiment's adjunct.

A list of the regiment's twenty-five other officers read like a

*Who's Who in the Abolition Movement.* With one well-placed shell, the Rebels could wipe out an entire generation of liberal Americans.

Waiting for the officers were twelve black recruits in red musicians' pants. Instead of rifles, they carried spikes.

Lincoln had thought of everything. Not only would the Blacks be good targets, they'd only be able to defend themselves in hand-to-hand combat.

While Robert fought with the War Department to have the soldiers issued blue pants and rifles, Governor Andrew got in touch with George L. Stearns. Stearns had once raised an army for John Brown and was known as an effective recruiter. "I'll get you your regiment," Stearns promised Andrew. "I'll succeed where the entire abolition movement has failed."

Stearns' first recruits were Frederick Douglass' sons, Lewis and Charles. The Hannibal Guards from Harlem signed up, and Otis Robinson brought back some of the three hundred men who'd been rejected by the New York Seventh. Other volunteers reported from New Jersey, Pennsylvania, Indiana, Illinois, Michigan, and every part of Canada. "I have worked anywhere from fourteen to eighteen hours a day," Stearns wrote Governor Andrew. "I have filled the West with my agents, convinced the railroads to give us discounts, written over five hundred letters, and borrowed over $10,000."

The real secret of Stearns' success, however, was his approach. Instead of tying to embarrass the Blacks into volunteering, Stearns let it be known that only the very finest specimens of physique and character would be considered. Within a month, men who would've been accepted in any other regiment had they been white were being rejected by the Massachusetts 54th. "I am doing a work that no one else can do," Stearns wrote Governor Andrew. "No one living could at this moment move the black man as I am moving him. Except the man who does not. What a response they would give to a call from Abraham Lincoln! Nothing would stop them. They would rush from every hole and corner, desert any occupation, make any sacrifice. These men are as capable as any whites of taking care of themselves and, on the whole, a lot more honest and brave."

Andrew asked Lincoln to give the call the Blacks wanted to

hear, but the president refused to support a project that had little chance of success. "Whatever will to fight the Blacks may have had when they first came to this country, has been beaten out of them by two hundred years of prejudice, discrimination, and slavery. For half the money it's costing me to raise these two regiments, I could ship all the soldiers and their families to Ile a Vache."

But the 54th didn't need Lincoln's help. One hundred recruits a week were showing up at the Readville training site. Seventy-five-year-old Rufus Brockway said his son was the cook for a company of New Hampshire infantry when he "got his nose barked and his lip broke by the Rebs at Bull Run." Now his grandfather was enlisting to see "if Johnny Reb can bark the old man's nose."

Sugar Bear Brown, whose brother was doing road work for the Union army in Kansas, showed up with twenty cousins. All under the age of seventeen. "Bigger done left me tuh work de blacksmith shop, but Ah knowed Bran do it good as me. So Bran do it till he fell lonesome. He toll Bluefront tuh do it and Bluefront toll Syke. Now deh women're workin it, but Ah spect dey be long any day now."

There was also a large number of escaped slaves. "Unlike the free Black," Robert wrote his mother, "the escaped slave has no pride or confidence. Three is no more soldier in him than there was a David in the raw marble before Michaelangelo took hold of it. They cover their heads with dirty strings, wear clothes that don't fit, walk with a moping gait, and I have yet to see one look me in the eye. They're usually big and strong, however, and those who pass our medical exam are shaved, scrubbed, and suited in clean, new uniforms. After a few weeks in the field, the change is almost complete. Yesterday's 'filthy nigger' is today's fighting soldier."

But what happened during those first weeks of camp worried some of the passengers who rode by on the Boston and Providence Line. They thought the Blacks were being mistreated and told Governor Andrew. Andrew told Robert.

"The freedmen have to rid themselves of their plantation manners," Robert replied. "They have to start feeling and acting like soldiers. They have to replace their servile bowing and scraping with the upright form of a fighter. They have to learn to be clean, to keep in step, and to handle guns. They have to understand that soldiers who sing, pray, dance, and prowl about all night can't be relied upon to fight well in the morning."

Knowing how upset his mother would be if she heard he mistreated Blacks, Robert wrote to her about what'd happened. "Any reports of cruelty simply aren't true," he said. "In fact, I treat these men far less harshly than I treated those in the Massachusetts Second."

Annie received a similar letter but with a different conclusion: "The men don't complain. They know I work them hard now so they will be able to protect themselves in battle later. Once they've proven themselves, I will be finished with them and in your arms forever."

Providing the weather didn't finish the men first. An early thaw had flooded the camp's low flat land, and everything that turned into mud during the day turned into ice as soon as the sun went down. Soaking wet soldiers froze through the night. Many of them became sick.

Robert feared the drills would be blamed and decided to ask the people of Readville for their help. The regiment had boosted the local economy; perhaps those who benefitted would return the favor.

Not only did the townspeople send enough clothes and supplies to fill the needs of three regiments, many of the donations had notes attached to them. One blanket announced it "was carried by Milly Aldrich, 93, down hill and up hill, one and a half miles, to be given to a black soldier." A card pinned to a quilt read: "My son is in the army. Whomever is made warm by this quilt, which took me six days and most all of six nights, let him remember his own mother's love." "This pillow," wrote another woman, "belonged to my little boy, who died resting on it. It is precious to me, but I give it to you." On a pair of woolen socks, a child embroidered, "These were knit by a little girl. I hope they help a black soldier. "This is a poor gift," read the label on a box containing bandages, "but it is all I have. Already gave my husband and my boy. I have nothing left."

By the end of March, the regiment's ranks were full, and all but a few of the soldiers were back on their feet. A thousand strong, they drilled three times a day, while Robert gave progress reports to the Black Committee, held a reception for The Wives of the Black Committee, spoke at a commemoration for Cripsus Attucks, and wrote countless letters to Annie.

They decided to marry in New York before the regiment left Boston, but a fight broke out between Sarah and Annie's mother over whether Robert should wear his uniform to the wedding. Sarah claimed her son was a soldier, he should look like one. Mrs. Haggarty said she didn't want to be reminded of the war and, since she was paying for the ceremony, she didn't think it was asking too much of Robert to wear a morning coat.

No one asked Robert what he wanted to wear.

George Stearns, meanwhile, was still sending volunteers to Readville. Governor Andrew commended the hard-working recruiter but wrote that he was against raising another regiment. The first one had been too much trouble.

Stearns wired that he had two hundred men toward a Massachusetts 55th. "What shall I do with them?"

Andrew said he'd give Stearns four weeks to raise eight hundred more.

Stearns sent a thousand.

# XV
## BOSTON

On April 30th, Robert boarded the overnight steamer for New York. He'd earned whatever rest the quiet, moonlit voyage offered him, but he couldn't sleep. He and Annie were going to marry in two days, and his mind raced with the conversations he imagined them having on their honeymoon. He would tell her everything that was important to know about the 54th: how there were more officers than soldiers the first day in camp, how the large number of volunteers had enabled him to select the best recruits, how they survived the winter, and how he'd changed them from a mass of men into the best fighting unit ever to march under the American flag.

Robert knew Annie had heard all of this before in his letters, but telling her in person would be different. For one thing, his feelings about the regiment had changed over the past few weeks. When the 54th was first organized, all he thought about was the day he'd resign. He even took a secret pleasure in the abolitionists' early inability to recruit volunteers and, for a while, wondered if there was ever going to be a black regiment. But there was, and everything he did in Readville was weighed against the misery of his separation from Annie. His attitude changed, however, during the struggle of the winter. The soldiers' stoicism, the townspeople's support, and the regiment's progress had brought him closer to his work. He still looked forward to the day he would retire with Annie, but he also wanted to do right by the regiment.

Annie didn't have any trouble sleeping the night of April 30th. She was exhausted. All winter long, she'd been making preparations for the wedding. She hadn't been too excited about the idea of getting married in New York, but there was no hotel in Lenox big enough to hold all the people Sarah wanted to invite. She was proud of her only son and wanted to show him off. In his uniform.

Annie was proud of Robert too, but, like her mother, she thought a morning coat was more appropriate. And she told him so. Marrying Robert was as much an extension of her life work as the war was his mother's; there was no reason why her wedding shouldn't be just the way she wanted it.

For the most part, it was. Flowers burst from the window boxes that decorated Fifth Avenue's brownstones, birds sang from the budding trees that lined Washington Square, and a brilliant sunlight gently illuminated the dark interior of Ascension Church. Annie appeared radiant in her mother's wedding gown, while Robert, though he brought his uniform, showed up in a morning coat.

After the ceremony, the couple climbed into a carriage and led a small army of friends and relatives to the Fifth Avenue Hotel on 23rd Street. Robert entertained Annie along the way with a story about Sergeant Carney. Carney had been named the regiment's color bearer because, when he enlisted, he said he'd worked as a "colored guard."

Annie asked Robert what he thought of the lovely music being orchestrated by the squeaks in their carriage's wheels and the clatter of the horse's hoofs on the pavement.

Robert said it was nice, but there was a soldier in the 54th who could make the sound of horses' hoofs by slapping his cheeks with the palms of his hands and blowing air through his mouth. Another soldier could play "John Brown's Body" by banging his fingernails on his teeth.

Annie asked Robert when he had turned in his colonel's uniform for a ringmaster's.

That shut him up. At least through dinner. But he started in again on the train to Lenox. One of the soldiers had written a song for the regiment:

> Fremont told them, when it first begun,
> To save the Union, and how to get it done.
> But Kentucky swore so hard, Old Abe had his fears,
> Till every hope was lost but the black Volunteers.
>
> McClellan went to Richmond with thousands brave.
> "Without the niggers, the Union we will save."
> Mac had his way, and the Union's still in tears.
> *Now* they call for help from the black Volunteers.
>
> So rally, boys, rally. Never mind the past.
> We've a road to travel, but our days' coming fast.
> God is for the right, and we have no need to fear.
> For the Union will be saved by the black Volunteers.

Annie stood up.
"What's the matter?"
"I'm leaving."
"What do you mean, you're leaving? Where are you going?"
"To preserve my wedding day."
"Huh?"
"This morning, Robert, we were married in the most magnificent church in New York. We rode in a hansom cab on the most beautiful day of the year to the city's most elegant hotel. We sat at a table overflowing with the best silver, china, and crystal that money could buy. We danced under chandeliers that made stars seem ordinary. Do you think that all happened by chance? I worked for months to make May 2nd, 1863, the most perfect day of your life and what do I get in return: stories about what a good time you've been having with your ridiculous niggers. How can you be so insensitive?"

Robert was dumbfounded.
"You had no idea, did you?"
Robert didn't.
And Annie could see that he didn't. "I don't know who is worse: you or your mother," she said as she stormed out of the cabin.

Robert's first impulse was to follow her, but he held himself back. If he chased after Annie now, he'd be running after her every time they had an argument. Not that this was an argument. He hadn't even said anything. But whatever it was, she'd walked out and she wasn't going to get way with it. If she could walk out, she could walk back in. All he had to do was sit and wait.

In another car, Annie wondered how Robert could have changed so much. Except for that one time at Susie's wedding, he'd always been so good. Even when he was lonely or not feeling well, his letters were filled with longing for her. Now he was in better spirits than she'd ever seen, and she didn't feel nearly as close to him. He'd always been a little self-centered, a little too prone to striking poses, perhaps, but he'd never been so insensitive as to make her suspect their wedding wasn't as important to him as the day his noncommissioned officers received their swords. What had happened?

Robert asked himself the same question. He tried to figure out where Annie had learned to walk out of a room like that. Was she the same person who had held him in her arms at Susie's wedding? A girlfriend of Heinrich's once walked out on him, and he never saw her again. He said women who walked out on men couldn't be trusted. Every time they were in a situation they didn't like, they would leave. And where did that leave the man? Constantly worrying about hurting their feelings. In short, dishonest. The man couldn't say what he really felt because he couldn't trust someone who responded to the truth by running away from it. "Anytime a woman walks out of a room," he told Robert, "let her go. She's better off gone, and so are you."

These were not the thoughts Robert hoped to find comfort in, but he couldn't get them out of his mind. What would happen to him and Annie if he couldn't trust her to let him be himself?

He didn't know. But now was neither the time nor the place to worry about it. First, he had to get Annie back. Then they had to talk.

Annie was pleased to see Robert searching the train for her. His face wore an anxious expression, and she realized she may have overreacted to his enthusiasm for the regiment. He had, after all, a right to be proud of his accomplishments. Why hadn't she seen that?

Without waiting for an answer, Annie rushed into her husband's arms. He held her and apologized—even though he thought she was in the wrong—and led her back to their cabin. Annie said she was sorry, too—though she knew the whole thing was his fault—and let him kiss her on the cheek. By the time they reached Lenox, all was forgiven and some had been forgotten.

The Haggartys had given their farm to Robert and Annie for a honeymoon, but the newlyweds were there only a few days when a telegram arrived from Governor Andrew: "Regiment assigned to South Carolina. Prepare to leave at once."

Several days later, the Massachusetts 54th formed a line outside of the Providence Depot in Boston. Several hundred officers from the city's police force were there just in case there was trouble. A regiment of state militia hid in reserve.

But there would be no trouble. The thousands of people who lined the parade route had come to cheer, not jeer, the 54th. Many pressed small parcels of food into the soldiers' hands.

Robert rode a blinding white charger and carried his unsheathed sword at his side. "He seemed to me both beautiful and awful," John Greenleaf Whittier later wrote. "Like an angel of God come down to lead the host of freedom to victory."

On Essex Street, the "host of freedom" saw William Lloyd Garrison standing on Wendell Phillips' balcony with a bust of John Brown in his arms. Tears were streaming down his face.

Frederick Douglass was also there. Through no fewer tears than Garrison's, he told the soldiers they were the country's symbol of freedom and equality.

A handful of members from the Somerset Club agreed. As the regiment passed by under their window, they drew its curtains. A liberal faction opened them, but the conservatives retaliated. Back and forth the curtains flew. Sergeant John Dwight explained to those around him that rich people had their own ways of cheering. Later that afternoon, the liberals resigned their memberships and formed the Union Club.

On Beacon Street, Robert raised his sword in honor of Annie and his mother, who were waving flags from the balcony of the old Sturgis home. Annie said Robert looked the very flower of grace and chivalry.

Sarah said Robert didn't just *look* it.

Entering the Boston Common, the 54th passed before the Black Committee, and Governor Andrew presented Sergeant Carney with two flags. The first, a gift from Francis and Sarah Shaw, was a white banner with Liberty carrying Loyalty and Unity in her arms. The second, a blue pennant bearing a white cross, was given by the Sturgis family in honor of Harry Russell.

"These flags will never touch the ground," Sergeant Carney promised Governor Andrew.

The governor then began a long speech about how his personal honor would rise or fall with the 54th. Robert tried to listen, but the huge crowds distracted him. He wondered if Professor Rawlinson was watching. Seven years had passed since Rawlinson had asked who from Harvard's Class of 1860 would make rather than read about history. The 54th was Robert's answer.

"Defenders of the downtrodden!" Governor Andrew told the men. "You have been given an opportunity to strike a blow for your whole race. By raising your country's flag—yours now as well as ours—and combating those who oppose it, you also strike at the shackles that bind your black brothers in the Rebel states."

"Though the greater number of men are not from this state," Robert told the governor, "they will fight as though they were. They will prove that those who have trusted the honor of Massachusetts to a black regiment have not made a mistake."

Sarah Shaw made her statement at Battery Wharf: she handed a Bible to each soldier as he boarded the ship that would take him to South Carolina. In each Bible she'd underlined, "The truth shall make you free."

Then she told Robert, "Death can take me before you are out of sight, and I will have no regrets."

Robert thanked his mother for all she'd done for him and the regiment. "If these men help the country and their race," he said, "you will share in their glory."

# XVI
# DARIEN

THE SOUTHERN DEPARTMENT'S MAIN OBJECTIVE WAS CHARLESTON. A Union blockade had cut off the city's sea routes as early as 1861, but several attempts to capture the war's birthplace had failed. Accurate Rebel intelligence, no support from the mainland, and Charleston's six impregnable harbor batteries were the reasons why. But Lincoln—who believed symbolic victories were often more devastating than tactical ones—wanted Charleston, not excuses. If General David Hunter couldn't take the city, the president would find someone who could.

These were strong words for Lincoln to use on a friend and former Chief of the White House Guards, but Hunter seemed to be increasingly more interested in his own popularity than the war. His only action since taking over the department was the capture of a small garrison on Cockspur Island. Lincoln had no objection to this—the Union could always use another island as a base for men and supplies—but one island in a year and a half left something to be desired. And so had Hunter's decision to free all the slaves in Georgia, Florida, and South Carolina six months before the president made *his* proclamation. The Confederacy didn't take the decree seriously and Lincoln disavowed it, but the damage was done: Hunter became the new darling of the Northern radicals.

And he continued to court their favor. When the First South Carolina Colored Volunteers were ordered to be formed under his command, Hunter asked the Reverend Thomas Wentworth Higginson to be the regiment's colonel. Higginson was famous in abolition circles for his plot to kidnap Governor Wise of Virginia and hold him in exchange for John Brown. When Brown was hanged, Higginson gave the money he'd raised for the kidnapping to James Montgomery. Montgomery wanted to blow up the jail where Brown's raiding party was being held, but the prisoners talked him out of it. They'd seen enough killing.

Not Montgomery. He was one of the first officers commissioned in the war and quickly developed a reputation for burning and hanging. When Higginson took over the First South Carolina, he named Montgomery his lieutenant colonel and chief recruiter.

Interpreting the word "volunteer" loosely, Montgomery recruited more men than George Stearns and all his agents combined. And at almost no cost to the government. He even had a name for his method: "bagging." Its definition lay somewhere between coercion and kidnapping.

Under Montgomery's direction, hundreds of Blacks were bagged wherever they were found. At home, on the road, in the fields, even in church. Many of those in the First hadn't said goodbye to their families. Others didn't know they'd be paid or given furloughs, and a few thought they were being sent to Cuba for having worked on plantations after Lincoln declared the slaves free.

Montgomery didn't care. These Blacks would be fighting for their own people. They were the ones who'd benefit from his methods. He was only helping them help themselves.

But Montgomery also benefitted. By the time the Massachusetts 54th arrived, he had assumed command of the Second South Carolina Colored Volunteers and was busy bagging volunteers for a Third. Hunter placed Robert under the command of Higginson and Montgomery. All the Blacks and abolitionists could be together, and the 54th's young colonel could learn something from his older and more experienced superiors.

Higginson, who was a friend of Governor Andrew, had been looking forward to meeting Robert and thanking him in person for the spy's letter he'd mailed when he was stationed in Virginia.

Robert asked if Higginson had recognized the spy's handwriting.

"It was disguised, but the information he gave enabled us to narrow our suspects to two."

"What did you do?"

"I killed them both," Montgomery volunteered.

Robert didn't know what to say. He'd seen violence among the uneducated soldiers, but Montgomery wasn't from the lower classes. He was a hero of the abolition movement. An innocent man's blood was on his hands.

"War isn't Harvard," Montgomery explained when he saw the expression on Robert's face. "If the Rebels refuse to change their ways, they must be swept away like the Jews of old." There was nothing extreme or strident in Montgomery's voice when he said this. In fact, everything from forbidding his men to smoke, swear, or drink to hanging reluctant volunteers was discussed in the same even tone. "Have any trouble forming the regiment?" he asked Robert.

"Not with the Blacks."

Higginson laughed knowingly, but Montgomery just smiled. He didn't like people who *tried* to be funny. "How do you think your men will hold up against whites?"

"They can fight better than most, but I think they could be placed between two fires the first time they see action."

Placing untried soldiers between the enemy and a force that prevented their retreat was a common practice, but Higginson didn't believe in it. He said it wasn't a Christian thing to do. "I can understand your concern," he assured Robert, "but once you've been under fire with the Blacks as I have, all your fears disappear."

"If your men run, Harvard, it won't be because they're cowards," Montgomery added.

"All I want is a chance for the regiment to prove itself," Robert told his commanders.

Montgomery suggested Robert join him in the morning for an expedition up the Altamaha River. "Take two companies. It won't be much of an outing, but your soldiers will destroy a major supply center and recruit some of their brothers for the cause."

The job of protecting the Altamaha River belonged to a detachment of thirty men from the 20th Georgia Cavalry. They were no match for the hundreds of soldiers in Montgomery's raiding parties, but their captain, W. A. Lane, had been watching the Yankees steal, loot, and burn long enough. What they needed was a taste of their own medicine.

While building his force up to a company of one hundred, Lane gradually removed the slaves within easy reach of Montgomery. Then he let it be known that the large Pierce Butler plantation outside of Darien was sending supplies to Charleston. If Montgomery was the kind of man Lane thought, he wouldn't be able to resist the easy pickings.

And so it was with a grim glee that Rebel pickets noticed Montgomery's raiding ships make their way up the Altamaha River.

From the deck of *The Princess*, Robert watched the lush Georgian landscape slip quietly by. Everything he could see once belonged to Pierce Butler. Robert recalled Fanny Kemble's description of her husband's land, but he didn't think he'd ever see it. Especially under these circumstances.

Ten years had passed since he threw himself at Fanny on the Isle of Capri. What a fool he'd been to listen to all her talk—how doing the right thing was easy because it didn't require any sensitivity. If anything, it made a person *more* sensitive. Had he gotten married and moved to California with Annie, he would have been miserable knowing he'd let down his family and the Union. Commanding the 54th wasn't easy, but it taught him a few things about what Blacks were up against. Talk about doing the right thing! These poor bastards were willing to die or be enslaved so people they didn't know could be free.

He wished Fanny could see him now. He'd tell her a thing or two. She hadn't even gotten the landscape on her own husband's plantation right. There were no butterflies flickering like flowers or gorgeous birds darting from boughs like winged jewels. According to the captain, the whole place was overrun with snakes and alligators.

Robert took back what he said about the landscape when the steamer came within sight of Darien. It was easily the most beautiful town he'd seen since he left Europe.

An old woman with a blunderbuss stood on the wharf.

Montgomery, thinking he'd have some fun with her, asked if she was a Confederate as his steamer pulled up to the pier.

"I'm a Methodist," she said, raising her blunderbuss.

"Well, my war is with Confederates."

The soldiers laughed at what they mistook for wit.

The woman cocked her gun.

"Nevertheless," Montgomery hastened to add, "I can't exactly classify you as a noncombatant . . ."

The woman fired.

Soldiers hit the ground everywhere and Montgomery's hat flew into the air. But the colonel kept his feet. Calmly, almost leisurely, he withdrew his revolver, took aim, and shot the woman in her chest. "Justice makes no allowance for age," he told Robert. "Let's scout the town, Harvard."

Robert, who was confused and troubled by what just happened, hesitated. He'd seen enough dead grandmothers for one day.

Montgomery misinterpreted Robert's behavior. "Don't worry," he said. "If the Rebels try something, we'll be caught between two fires."

Robert wished he knew what Montgomery had against him. He realized he shouldn't have suggested putting the Blacks between two fires, but it was a common practice and no reason for Montgomery to make him feel foolish.

Established by Governor Oglethorpe, the founder of Georgia, and settled by Scots from Inverness, Darien was the state's financial center. Oak trees shaded homes that dated back to colonial times, the town square was marked by three white churches, and in the middle of the common was a memorial to those who defended Darien against a Spanish invasion in 1742.

"Harvard?"

"Yes, sir."

"You like this town?"

"It's very pretty, sir."

"I want you to sack it."

"Sir?"

"I want you to sack it."

"But, sir, the *Instructions for Armies in the Field* prohibits the seizure of any material that can't be used in camp."

"Are you questioning my orders, Harvard?"

"No, sir."

"Then you're calling me a thief."

"No, sir."

"What then?"

"Nothing, sir. I just wanted to make sure what you wanted taken."

"Everything."

Robert ordered his men to carry whatever lumber, resin, cotton, and wheat they could find to the ships, but Montgomery extended the list to include anything the soldiers could lay their hands on.

A parade of sofas, tables, chairs, paintings, pianos, mirrors, and carpets soon made its way to the wharf.

"Harvard?"

"Yes, sir."

"The cavalry and I are going to bag some niggers."

"Yes, sir."

"And I don't want you spoiling the men's fun while I'm gone. If they can sleep better on beds and sofas than on the ground, they'll be in better shape to fight."

"Yes, sir."

"You don't sound convinced."

"I didn't say that, sir."

"Not everyone is born with a silver spoon in his mouth, Harvard. Some people had to work for whatever they have and some had to work for others. The paintings, pianos, and everything else belongs to these troops. Their sweat as slaves made this town what it is. They deserve a little something in return."

"Yes, sir."

"One more thing. Once you have everything loaded on the ships?"

"Yes, sir?"

"I want you to burn it."

"The booty?"

"The town."

"But the *Instructions for Armies in* . . . "

"Damn the *Instructions*, Harvard. Mention them to me again and I'll shoot you."

What had begun as a festival now turned into an orgy of chaos and destruction. First the warehouse, market place, and sawmill were set on fire. Then the homes. Seventy-five of them went up like matchsticks. Everything that had been made by man was burned to the ground, and any animals that hadn't been taken on board were shot.

Montgomery's cavalry, meanwhile, wasn't doing much better than the animals left behind in Darien. Just outside of Butler plantation, the whole countryside had come alive with Rebels. Montgomery was hit twice in the first volley, and a third of his men went down with him. Those still on their horses tried to escape, but they found their retreat blocked off. Completely surrounded, the cavalry took whatever cover they could find.

Robert knew from the sudden burst of rifle fire that Montgomery had been ambushed. Ordering the First South Carolina to defend the ships, he rushed the 54th to the rescue.

Two fleeing survivors told them to go back. "It's a sure death," they told Robert.

Farther down Butler Plantation Road, another survivor told the troops the entire party would be wiped out by the time the 54th got there. "Go back while you still can. The whole day has been lost."

Robert told his men that their day had not yet begun and ordered them to form two lines. If the Confederates had Montgomery pinned down—and all the shots from the same direction indicated they did—the 54th could cover the cavalry and outflank the Rebels at the same time.

Captain Lane was surprised when he saw his men dropping about him. He'd been having such a good time taking target practice on Montgomery's cavalry, he overestimated the time it would take the soldiers at the wharf to reach the battle. Now he was the one in danger of being surrounded.

Soldiers in the 54th wanted to chase the Rebels when they withdrew after only a few shots, but Robert wouldn't let them. Getting all Montgomery's men to safety was more important.

But the men bristled at having to stay in line. Some, like Private Lew Green, would run forward, fire, fall back, reload, and rush out again. "Nowza time to go afta dem," Sergeant James Dwight shouted. "Whyn't we git Johnny Reb whilst he's . . . "

Dwight hit the ground with a bullet in his neck.

And Green didn't come back.

The Confederates had regrouped on the other side of Montgomery and were filling the air with lead.

Robert ordered his men to hold their positions. This meant exposing themselves to the enemy's fire, but what was left of the cavalry was able to pull back.

"Nothing you ever do will equal the honor your men just won for you," Montgomery told Robert. "Now I will make them immortal."

Heavily outnumbered and short on ammunition, the Rebels fired one final blast and ran for their lives as they saw Montgomery bearing down on them.

Montgomery chased the bushwackers as far as Butler Plantation. There was something he could use more than a body count: an abandoned train. "Have your men load up all the wounded," he told Robert.

In spite of carrying three bullets and having lost enough blood to fell another man, Montgomery insisted on starting the train himself, but he created so much steam the engine's flue collapsed.

Montgomery wouldn't be denied, however. He was determined to carry his cavalry in a train even if he had to order the 54th to push it.

Which is exactly what happened.

Robert's men had already plundered and burned a town, run to the rescue of the cavalry, fought in their first skirmish, combed the woods for survivors, and loaded them on a train. Now they were ordered to push an engine and four cars full of cavalry from Butler Plantation to Darien. They had all they could do to push themselves, but they also knew how many cavalry would die if they were transported any other way.

Only the line to Darien wasn't a direct one. It ran through two other plantations first. Not only that but Montgomery wanted the tracks torn up behind them.

The train didn't reach Darien until morning. Nearly half Robert's soldiers were without shoes. Their feet bled from the splinters they'd picked up from the railway ties. Many suffered burns from the ropes they used for towing.

As the soldiers from the First South Carolina carried the wounded to a transport, those in the 54th fell to the ground as if they'd been dropped from the sky. Not one had ever felt closer to death, but there were no stragglers and every soldier still carried the gun he'd been issued.

# XVII
## OAKLANDS

ROBERT WROTE FIRST TO ANNIE, THEN TO HIS MOTHER. He called the burning and looting of Darien the most "abominable work" he'd ever seen. "If word of this gets out, the Blacks will be characterized as barbarians. But what can I do about it? I either obey Montgomery and shame myself or refuse to go on any more forays and be courtmartialed."

Annie told Robert to resign his commission and come home. "If that's the way Blacks fight, they don't deserve to be soldiers."

Sarah told her son to be patient. She'd forwarded his letter to the War Department.

But Secretary of War Stanton didn't take the letter too seriously. He asked Montgomery for a report and believed everything Montgomery told him. The raid was costly—three officers wounded, thirteen enlisted men dead, sixty-three wounded, and eight missing—but Montgomery had repulsed the enemy, disabled a steam engine, torn up ten miles of track, destroyed a major supply center to Charleston, and confiscated enough cotton, resin, wood, and salt pork to fill the Southern Department's needs for a month. Perhaps he'd been slightly overzealous in destroying property that could be used against Northern armies, but the sawmill and warehouse weren't as important as the soldiers' safety and morale. If Shaw had pursued the ambushers instead of just scaring them off, Montgomery not only would have controlled the fire, Captain Lane would be pushing up grass now.

But that's not how the people of Darien saw it. In a ledger that survived the blaze, they found the names of some of the soldiers who destroyed the town. Heading the list was Robert Gould Shaw.

The Mayor of Darien sent the names and several eyewitness accounts to Secretary Stanton. When Stanton didn't reply, he sent a copy of his complaint to the *New York Tribune*. The story soon appeared in other newspapers throughout the North and South.

The news that he was being held responsible for what happened at Darien frustrated, discouraged, and hurt Robert. He wanted to resign.

"You'll do nothing of the sort," Sarah wrote. "You've survived too many bullets to be taken out by a pen. The careless recruit who wrote your name in the ledger was expressing his admiration of you. To resign now would only confirm what the newspapers are saying."

Robert tore up his letter of resignation, but Sarah had only begun to write. None of the war's other atrocities had been given nearly so much attention, and this one would've died quickly, too, if the regiment hadn't been black. Lincoln had obviously suppressed the South Carolina's role in the raid and exempted Montgomery from any responsibility to discredit the free Blacks and further his colonization program.

When Lincoln read what the abolitionists were saying about him, he summoned the Secretary of War. Stanton suggested getting rid of both Montgomery and Shaw. The former was reckless and the latter didn't know when to keep his mouth shut.

The president agreed, but Shaw was an abolitionist—that meant votes—and Montgomery won battles—that meant support for the war. He couldn't get rid of them without jeopardizing the more important reasons for their being there.

"But you can't ignore the situation," Stanton pointed out. "If these atrocities aren't answered for, the Rebels will reciprocate on their own terms."

Lincoln fired Hunter.

Hunter demanded an explanation. It wasn't his fault the

Rebels attacked and the fire got out of control. Why was the president doing this to him? Weren't they still friends?

Lincoln, who had a reputation for plain speaking, wrote Hunter that his removal was "for no reasons which convey any imputation upon your known energy, efficiency, and patriotism; but for causes which seemed sufficient, while they were in no degree incompatible with the respect and esteem in which I have always held you as a man and officer."

Robert was relieved to hear Hunter had been dismissed, but his replacement, General Quincy Adams Gillmore, did nothing to control Montgomery's behavior. One week after Gillmore's arrival, Montgomery hanged a deserter without courtmartial and shot a recruit who disobeyed his order not to sing after taps.

Annie couldn't have cared less about Hunter or Montgomery. She'd gotten her hopes up about Robert's coming home and was disappointed when he decided not to resign. She told him he shouldn't have mentioned resigning if he intended to change his mind.

Robert reminded Annie that she was the one who'd suggested resigning. He was sorry she was disappointed but, as his wife, she also had a responsibility to the regiment. Once the men had proven themselves, he'd be on the next train to Lenox.

It wasn't the first time he'd lied to her. He wanted the soldiers to prove themselves all right, but right now Robert didn't want to get any closer to Lenox than Oaklands.

An abandoned plantation on the other side of St. Helena, Oaklands had become the center of an abolitionist project to provide work and education for black refugees. While former slaves worked in fields for government wages, their children learned to read and write in the mansion. Robert first visited the center after he returned from Darien—his parents had pressed him for a report—but he'd returned to the plantation every day since. Oaklands was where Charlotte Forten lived.

Charlotte was one of eight teachers hired to instruct the black children. She was smart, beautiful, and dedicated. Robert was first attracted to her because she was warm like Fanny Kemble without being silly. She was also high-purposed without being severe like his mother. There wasn't anything of Annie in her. Charlotte wasn't even white.

After Robert told Charlotte about what'd happened in Darien, she introduced him to some of Pierce Butler's former slaves.

The slaves told Robert that "Massa Butler" was a good man, but he drank and gambled too much. Eventually, he had to sell the plantation and all his slaves. Over four hundred men, women, and children were separated from their families. After "Massa Lincoln" freed them, some of the slaves escaped to St. Helena. They wanted to know if Robert would bring their children back.

In spite of his being an abolitionist and commander of the 54th, this was the first time Robert ever talked with any Blacks as people. They'd always been part of the great collective cause. Now, thanks to Charlotte, his involvement had become personal.

Charlotte grew up in Philadelphia. The city didn't allow Blacks in its schools, and Charlotte learned to read and write at her grandfather's house. She carried her books wrapped in paper so the police wouldn't see them. Her grandfather, a famous sailmaker and abolitionist, was impressed with how quickly she learned and made arrangements for her to attend the state normal school in Salem, Massachusetts. She didn't want to leave her family, but now she was glad she had. Charlotte wished everyone could be as happy as she'd been since coming to St. Helena.

Robert and Charlotte attended service together the Sunday after they met and explored an abandoned plantation in the afternoon. Not far from the mansion, they discovered a chapel almost hidden by the trees and moss. Robert promised to repair the building in time for a Fourth of July service.

Robert liked Charlotte more every time he saw her. She wasn't like the other women in his life. Whereas Annie would tell him everything was all right and his mother would tell him he was all wrong, Charlotte helped him understand his problems and do something about them. She said he couldn't remove the guilt he felt about Darien, but he could redeem himself by leading the 54th to victory in a real battle. Similarly, he couldn't assuage the guilt he felt over Harry's death, but he could prevent more deaths by keeping his soldiers out of unnecessary danger. As a colonel, he had that power.

Robert once mentioned Charlotte to Annie in a letter, but he wrote about little else to his mother. "Can you imagine anything more amazing than Miss Forten holding a colored abolitionist meeting on a South Carolina plantation? God is not very far from Oaklands."

Charlotte was also quite taken with Robert. "There is something in him that is finer, more exquisite than one often sees in a man," she wrote in her diary the day they visited the abandoned plantation. "How full of life and hope and lofty aspirations he is." After their next meeting: "I could feel my heart beat as he helped me on my horse and arranged the folds of my riding skirt. The nobleness of his soul shines through his face."

Robert saw his nobility reflected in Charlotte's face every time she looked at him, and he didn't feel very good about it. He had yet to tell her he was married. When they met, it hadn't seemed important. Later, as he became more attracted to her, he didn't want to give her a reason to distance herself from him. Now they were becoming close in a way that compromised his fidelity to Annie. He had to tell Charlotte the truth.

But something happened that kept Robert from seeing Charlotte when he planned; he became a hero.

# XVIII
## St. Helena

Payday never meant much to Robert. Except for a few years following the Crash of 1857, he always had more money than he could spend. The same was true for most of the officers.

The recruits were a different story. Unlike the other soldiers in the Union army, they hadn't received hundred dollar bounties to tide them over until their training was complete. They'd enlisted knowing they would receive half bounties only if they survived the war. They also agreed to have money taken from their pay that white troops received as an allowance. Four months and not a penny of income later, most of the men's wives and families had moved in with relatives or the families of other soldiers. Some, like Sergeant Swail's family, were in the poorhouse.

But this didn't stop Lincoln from reducing the soldiers' promised pay of thirteen dollars a month to ten. That was less than government laborers earned.

The soldiers wouldn't stand for it.

And neither would Robert. He told the paymaster to give the men their full thirteen dollars.

The paymaster said he had his orders.

Robert said his men weren't moving until they were paid the money entitled them.

When General Gillmore heard what was going on, he sent a

man who knew how to handle Blacks, to put them back in their place: Montgomery.

"Men of the 54th," Montgomery told the soldiers. "You have yet to prove yourselves as men. A few of you have been under a little fire, but you have yet to attack or repulse an enemy. Nor should you expect to be treated the same as whites. Anyone listening to your shouting and singing can see how ignorant and inferior you are. Nevertheless, I am a friend of the nigger. I was the first in the country to free my slaves and the first to employ niggers in the army. I was out in Kansas. I was short of men. I had a lot of niggers and a lot of mules, and you know how well niggers and mules go together. I enlisted the niggers and made teamsters out of them. If you refuse to take your pay, you are guilty of insubordination and mutiny. You can be courtmartialed and shot. You light-colored niggers may think you're better than the others because you have white blood in you, but you're not. You're worse. If anything, you should get less for being bastards to your race. The Lord . . . "

"That's enough," Robert interrupted. "These men have every right to expect the money promised them. If you're not out of here in five minutes, I'll shoot you myself."

Montgomery had no idea he'd said anything offensive, but he wasn't the kind to avoid a confrontation. Especially with someone like Robert. "You threatening me, Harvard?"

Robert drew his pistol from its holster, cocked it, and aimed at Montgomery's chest. "I'm promising you."

Montgomery muttered something about Harvard and walked away.

The men didn't make a sound. They were shocked by what they'd just seen.

So was Robert, but he recovered enough of his composure to call a meeting of the regiment's officers: commissioned and non-commissioned.

Frederick Douglass' son, Lewis, was the first to speak. "When Mr. Stearns came to our home, he asked my father why Blacks didn't enlist more readily. If he'd been here today, he'd have his answer. We're continually being asked to do more for less, but all we ever get is less for more."

Robert said he hadn't called the meeting to listen to

complaints about the obvious. He planned to tell General Gillmore the soldiers wouldn't accept anything less than what they were entitled to, and he wanted his officers' reaction.

Theodore Tilton said his men had been expecting something like this and were ready to stack their arms.

Robert's lieutenant, Ned Hallowell, asked Tilton if he knew stacking arms was considered mutinous.

"Payin' us less den we wuz promised is treason."

"Mutiny is punishable by death."

"So be treason."

"You plan to kill your officers?"

"You plan tuh shoot deh entire regiment?"

Wilkie James, Robert's adjunct, had heard enough. "We're not going to get anywhere fighting each other. That's just what Lincoln wants. It's part of his plan to make us look bad."

"Well, he's not going to get away with it," Lewis exclaimed. "Colonel Shaw was right when he said anything less than we were promised is unacceptable."

"An how many of us do yuh think can go on livin' on nothin'?" Sergeant Swails countered. "All deh officers come from money. It's easy for dem tuh say deh pay is unacceptable. Dey don't have tuh live on no seven dollars a month."

"Ten," Hallowell corrected.

"Seven," said several soldiers at once. "Deh government's already takin three dollars from us for deh clothin'," Swails added.

Hallowell said he knew the money was important, but was it the soldiers' reason for joining the army? "How can you equate money with freedom?"

"Money is freedom," R. J. Simmons replied. "Sure we could've made more money at home. We didn't join for the money any more than you rich people did. But equal pay's the principle we hope to get equal rights by when the war's over."

"If we'd a listed for deh money," said Theodore Tilton, "we might well as take deh seven dollars. Buht we done come heah tuh make mens of ourselves and our race."

"You not black so you don't see deh ways of deh whites like we does," Sergeant Simmons continued. "By not payin' us the same as deh whites, Lincoln's tellin' us we cain't be Union soldiers. Aht seven dollars a month, we ain't even laborers."

"Why don't we talk about what we're going to do about the money?" Robert asked.

"I done told you," answered Tilton. "If mah men don't get whutz comin tah dem, dey be stackin."

"And if you get shot for it," asked Hallowell, "will your life have been worth the three dollars you lost?"

"Yessuh, cuz weel've dahd like men instead've livin' like labrers."

"Whutz so bad bout bein a labrer?" asked a soldier who hadn't spoken. "Most of us be labrers fore we be soldiers."

"Dass just how deh man wants you tuh think," Simmons explained. "Grateful fur what you get. Jes like Uncle Tom."

"Uncle Tom weren't so bad."

Robert interrupted. "This isn't getting us anywhere. The government has decided not to give you the money you were promised. I want to refuse anything less than you deserve, but can you live with that until the issue is resolved?"

Sergeant Swails wanted to know why the government would want to pay soldiers who would fight for free.

Robert couldn't say, but he knew the abolitionists would pressure Lincoln to give in.

"We's stackin," said Tilton.

"And I told you," said Hallowell, "you're going to be shot for it."

"An Ah toll you, you cain't shoot us all."

Robert tried to keep Tilton and Hallowell from getting out of hand. "If we're going to beat Lincoln, we're going to have to stick together."

The non-commissioned officers all looked at him. It was the first time Robert had associated himself with them and first time he'd come out openly against the president.

Lewis Douglass said he knew all but a few of the soldiers were destitute. "But if we gripe about money, Lincoln will only accuse us of being selfish and unpatriotic. *We* know its the principle that counts. So does he. But he's going to say we're doing whatever we decide for the money. We have to fight Lincoln in a way that can't be used against us. We've got to give up the money now to get the money later."

"Ah cain't do dat," said Swails. "Mah family's in deh poorhouse. All Ah heah from mah wife's how hungry dey all is. Ah cain't tell dem dey has tuh live on principle."

"It only be until the government admits we're not fightin for the money," Lewis explained.

"This all assumes that Lincoln cares about principles," Wilkie James cautioned. "He may use them against others, but does he hold any himself?"

Robert pointed out that it didn't matter. The men couldn't accept the seven dollars a month—that was an insult—and they couldn't stack arms or go home—that was treason. If they wanted to retain any sense of dignity and get what they deserved, they'd have to go on as they always had: not because of the Union but in spite of it. For as long as it took Lincoln to reverse his decision, they and their families would have to live on glowing accounts of battle, brave deeds, and self-respect.

# XIX
## St. Helena

ROBERT AND CHARLOTTE CELEBRATED THE FOURTH OF JULY with a service in the chapel they'd discovered on the abandoned plantation. One of Charlotte's students read the "Declaration of Independence," and a preacher asked Jesus for a "right smart charge of gunpowder to blow Johnny Reb back to shoes, the fatted calf, and the ways of the Union."

The people punctuated the preacher's prayer with shouts of "Yes!" and "Amen!" This excited the preacher more. His voice became shrill. The people began singing and dancing in the aisles. The preacher shouted that he could "see the Light!" Others saw it, too. A woman fainted but the people kept on dancing. Nothing was more important than singing and dancing and clapping and shouting and seeing the Light.

Robert moved to help the fallen woman, but Charlotte grabbed his hand and led him out of the chapel. "I know there are many ways in which the black people are still uncivilized," she said, "but they haven't had the same advantages as whites. The slaveholders shackled their minds as well as their bodies. It will take some time for the pagan rituals to fall away."

Robert said he'd enjoyed watching the people.

"You mean they amused you. Like freaks in a circus. You don't have to be polite. They disgust me, too. They don't realize that until they rid themselves of every African vestige and adopt the white man's civilization, they will remain an inferior race. True equality won't be achieved until the only difference is color."

Ordinarily, Robert would have agreed. Charlotte's philosophy was the same as that of most liberal whites who saw the slaves as a combination of noble savages and childlike candidates for civilization. The whole St. Helena project was a result of that thinking. But there was something in Charlotte's voice that made her sound as if she was being unfair and Robert told her so.

"Then let me put it another way. How would you feel if you saw your mother behaving that way? Or your wife?"

Robert should've known Annie was at the bottom of this. She'd been at the bottom of just about everything Charlotte said or did for days. But it hadn't started like that. The night he told her about Annie, all she cared about was Montgomery. Even when he told her that it wasn't Montgomery's way to have him arrested, she'd been more concerned for his safety than his marriage. Perhaps she hadn't wanted to think about it then. Well, she'd certainly thought about it since.

And so had he. His loss of affection for Annie troubled him, but he also craved Charlotte's company. Even the petty quarrels they'd been having had somehow become almost necessary. Yet every time they talked, things seemed to get more confused. So far they'd only kissed, but he could feel her desire and he knew Charlotte was not unaware of his.

Charlotte felt Robert's letter pressing against her heart as she waited for an answer about seeing his wife in a shout. He'd written to her the day he threatened to shoot Montgomery, telling her what a coward he'd been to keep his marriage a secret but assuring her of his affection at the same time. She understood how he felt and told him so when he showed up later that night. He hadn't planned on falling in love with another woman when he married Annie. It was only natural for him to be confused and upset.

But Robert had been confused and upset for more days now than Charlotte thought necessary, and he still seemed more interested in reassuring her than pursuing their passion. This, of course, had the opposite effect than he intended. Whenever they were together, she felt insecure and couldn't behave naturally. How could she help it? Until he broke the news of his marriage, she'd never felt more comfortable with a man. This thought and Robert's continued silence brought Charlotte back to the situation at hand. She could see that he was clearly struggling with himself. And equally as clear was the fact that *she* was losing. "Let's not fight," she said.

"I'm not fighting."

"What are you doing then?"

"I'm waiting for you to stop being disagreeable."

"I wasn't until you said I was unfair. You know as well as I do what makes Blacks want to scream and shout and shuffle in a ring. We've talked about it. If I'd given in to those impulses, I never would've learned to read and write, and you'd be no more attracted to me than you are to those people in the chapel."

Robert admitted Charlotte was different than most Blacks, but that wasn't why he was attracted to her. "I think you're the most beautiful, most accomplished woman I've ever known. And you have a vibrancy that makes most ordinary people look exhausted. I wish I had half your enthusiasm and dedication."

"You do. And what's more, you're sensible. You don't fly off the handle at every little thing. That's why I trust you to see us through this mess."

"You know I never expected anything like this to happen."

"I was pretty surprised myself."

"It's funny how fast things can change, isn't it?"

"Yes, but you're the same man who walked into my classroom, and I'm the same woman whose lap held your head after the confrontation with Montgomery."

"It's not easy being in a situation like this and knowing what's right."

"If any man knows what's right, Robert, it's you."

"It's just that I don't want anybody to get hurt."

"Do you mean Annie?"

"I mean you and Annie. All of us."

"You don't see us as a temporary thing, do you Robert? I don't know what I'd do if you did."

"Of course not. That's why I'm worried about what's going to happen. I'm afraid I'm playing with fire."

"Life is fire, Robert. Our life at any rate. That's why we're here and not in some cozy cottage in the Berkshires."

Robert let the remark pass. "You're so brave," he said.

"So are you."

"You won't change your mind about us, will you? You won't ever say we can't see each other."

"Never."

"Good. When shall we meet again?"

The next time was in the library of the officer's mansion. Robert had been feeling miserable about Annie and had gone two days without seeing Charlotte. When Charlotte had first said she loved him, everything was very clear in his own mind. She had taken the responsibility of declaring her affection; he had accepted the responsibility of seeing her through a phase. At least that's how he saw it now. She couldn't have helped falling in love with him. There couldn't have been more than a handful of attractive men on the island the whole time she was there. And the fact she was black probably didn't help. Most of the officers probably took her for a camp girl. She certainly didn't have a very high opinion of them. But now, having fallen in love with someone who could accept her for what she was, she needed his love to set her free from the tangle they'd gotten themselves into.

What at first seemed easy to control, however, soon got out of hand. How could he have anticipated his desire for Charlotte? How could he have prepared for the confusion that followed? How could he have known that what had brought them together wouldn't hold? Their relationship began falling apart almost as soon as they fell in love. That's when he decided to stop seeing her, but by then he'd also assumed the responsibility of managing their relationship.

The more Charlotte thought about it, the more she realized that Robert suited her more than anybody she'd ever met. Whatever other men there had been in her life just didn't compare. Robert had that special sense of authority and nobility that she needed to make her life complete. At first, she'd been a little uncertain about how to respond to Annie, but his assurances and sincerity gave her confidence. Even when Annie had become something of a nuisance, Charlotte's knowledge of herself, her estimation of Robert, and her trust in his affection gave her the strength to remain loyal to him. She owed him that much. It couldn't have been easy for a man like Robert to love her and live with the idea of a wife. Naturally, he felt guilty. But what she hadn't forseen was the power of that guilt. It was tearing him apart and, like the good man he was, he was trying to handle it all by himself. Well, she wasn't about to let him do that. If he wouldn't come to her, she would go to him. He'd declared his love for her, and she had a responsibility to protect him from the guilt that was destroying them.

"I think you should tell Annie," Charlotte said after she was shown into the library. "It's the only way to get rid of your guilt."

Robert had been afraid Charlotte would suggest this. Under the circumstances, it was the only decent thing to do, but he knew he couldn't hurt Annie like that.

"It was just an idea," Charlotte said when Robert didn't respond.

"We have to be responsible for Annie's feelings, too."

"I am. Don't you think she's going to be even more hurt later on? Losing you would be a terrible blow no matter when it came, but realizing you'd deceived her might be too much to bear. In a way, you're insulting her by not telling her how you feel."

"But what about how *you* feel? I can't burden you with the consequences of my deceit. You've already done more than I could ever expect."

"I want to help see you through this, Robert."

"I know. I just wish I wasn't so confused about what was right."

"Your letter didn't sound confused."

"I think better in my letters."

"Maybe you should write one to Annie."

"Maybe I should."

"I'm glad you agree. Oh, Robert, you have the sweetest expression when you're troubled."

"I know I have no right to ask this," he said, "but may I hold you for a moment? You've become so dear to me, and you've been so patient. I've simply got to hold you."

Charlotte placed her arms around Robert's neck and drew her body up against his. He closed his eyes and held on for a long, deep time. When they parted, they realized the door to the library had been opened. Someone else was in the room. Charlotte didn't know who she was.

But Robert did.

# XX
## Beaufort

ANNIE SHUT THE WINDOW AND CLIMBED BACK UNDER THE COVERS. Here she was in a poorly vented room in Beaufort, South Carolina, in the middle of July, and she'd come down with a chill. Well if that's all she came down with, she'd consider herself lucky. It wasn't every day that one's heart and life were broken. She'd seen it coming and was able to prepare herself, but the blow of actually seeing her husband in the arms of another woman had been more devastating than she'd imagined. It even led her to blame herself for what had happened. Perhaps if she hadn't been so anxious to marry Robert things would have been different. She wondered if he regretted having married her. How could he not? She was not clever or dedicated. And compared to him, she must have seemed pretty dull. Compared to Charlotte, she was nothing. Except she was white, and she would never forgive Robert for preferring a black woman.

But what if it wasn't like that? What if this Charlotte person really was in some kind of trouble and Robert was just helping her? It was possible. But that was no reason not to tell her. She'd felt so embarrassed when all Sarah talked about was Charlotte Forten. Charlotte Forten this and Charlotte Forten that. At first, she suspected Sarah of trying to make her feel guilty for not having followed Robert to war as a nurse but, when she saw the letters he'd written to his mother, she put two and two together and came up with three.

And yet, she still wanted to believe Robert had been telling the truth in the library. But looking back it seemed that Charlotte had done most of the talking. "So it's true," Annie had said when she saw them in each other's arms.

Charlotte wanted to know what was true.

Annie told her.

Charlotte denied it.

"Then why'd you close the door?"

"We were talking about something important. We didn't want anyone to hear."

"I saw how you were talking."

"We happened to be talking about you."

"How could I possibly doubt it?"

"If you don't believe me, ask your husband."

Annie looked at Robert, but he couldn't take his eyes off the floor. He muttered something that sounded like "That's true," or "It's the truth," but his voice was garbled as if his mouth had something in it.

"There," said Charlotte. "Are you satisfied now?"

"Quite" was all she could get out before she broke down and ran for the ferry to take her to Beaufort.

"Annie! Annie!"

It was Robert. She got out of bed and opened the door. He brushed by her into the room. "Annie. Listen. Whatever you saw isn't what you . . . "

"Don't," she interrupted. "You'll only make it worse."

"Make what worse?"

"Please, Robert. No more lies. They don't become you."

"But there's nothing between me and . . . "

"I know. All you do is talk. Well, you have a very strange way of conversing."

"Annie, there's been a misunderstanding."

"There's been nothing of the kind. I saw everything, and I promise you I won't stand in your way. So don't insult me by pretending something isn't true when it is."

"If you'd only let me explain. I love you. You're my wife. I admit I should've told you about what was going on. It was all my fault, but . . . "

"Don't bother explaining. There's nothing you can say. There's only one explanation for what I saw. It's over between you and me."

"But I haven't done anything. Nothing's changed between us. I wasn't having an affair. I swear I . . . "

"Robert, you're making me think less of you every time you open your mouth. Can't you see what you've done?"

"You can't know what you don't know, Annie."

"Oh, Robert, I loved and respected you so. How could you have sunk so low?"

"But I didn't *do* anything. That's what I'm trying to say. I deceived you a little I admit. It was wrong of me, and I promise never to do it again. But if you don't listen to me, you're going to ruin our marriage over a misunderstanding. What happened between me and Charlotte is not what you think. *She* fell in love with *me.*"

"That's not how your mother made it sound."

"What's my mother got to do with this?"

"She showed me your letters because I was lonely. She thought I'd enjoy reading them."

"Then she knows?"

"Not what I do."

"But you know *nothing*. That's what I want to explain. *Charlotte* fell in love with *me.*"

"Spare me the details. Those are for you and Charlotte to entertain yourselves with in the years to come."

"Will you please *listen*?" Robert begged as Annie shivered and climbed back into bed. "She fell in love with me. I was trying to help her get over it."

"I saw how hard you were trying in the library."

Robert didn't say anything. Whatever he tried would only be thrown back in his face.

"Are you saying you don't love her?"

"No—I love her—I guess, but not in the way you think."

"What does it matter what I think as long as you're in love? You're not the first man to leave his wife once he's become important. When you were a weak little captain and needed a shoulder to cry on, you loved me; but now that you're a colonel and have a regiment of your own you don't like being reminded of who you were when you were a captain. And that's who you see every time you think of me, isn't it? But Charlotte doesn't see the timid little captain. She only knows the big brave colonel who burned a defenseless town. And that's the way you want to keep her, isn't it? You don't want her to find out what you're really like. Well, I don't blame you. If I was a coward, I'd do exactly what you're doing. I guess I should be thankful it happened now and not later. No that it makes much difference. This kind of hurt doesn't go away after a few weeks. It lasts a whole lifetime. And there's nothing anyone can do to make it better."

"But Annie. Nothing's happened. There's nothing to be made better because nothing's been destroyed. Charlotte was infatuated. I was only trying to help her get over it. We were both worried about you."

"How very comforting to know. Well, let me tell you that your kind of concern disgusts me."

Robert gasped for breath. He wanted to say something, but all he could think about was his last few minutes with Charlotte. He'd remarked that she seemed very calm under the circumstances. He meant it as a compliment, but she took it as an insult. She said she was very upset, but someone had to keep the situation under control. All Robert had done was look guilty.

"But we are guilty."

"What?"

"We are guilty. We were caught red-handed."

"Robert, you know sometimes you really irritate me. You entered this relationship knowing something like this would happen if you didn't tell Annie the truth, but you were so worried about doing what was right you only perpetuated what was wrong. And just now when you had the chance to straighten everything out, you didn't do anything."

"Charlotte, please keep your voice down. There are other officers in the mansion. They might hear."

"What do I care about the other officers? If you'd been half the man you led me to believe you were, we wouldn't be having this conversation."

"Well, fighting isn't going to get us anywhere. We've got to think of something."

"You're right about that," she said. "Meeting your wife like that was quite a shock."

"Do you think she knew?"

"No. It was probably just a coincidence. But you'll have some explaining to do. Just don't lose your nerve. Do what you know is right."

"I hope I can."

"Poor boy, you really are a coward, aren't you? You know sometimes I think it would've been better if we'd just gone to bed and not wasted all this time with talk that doesn't lead anywhere."

"You're probably right, but I couldn't do that knowing . . . "

"I know. But don't worry. I'm not going to ask you for anything now. Go find your wife and hope she understands."

It didn't take long to trace Annie to Beaufort. Robert was surprised to learn, however, that she'd reserved the room from Lenox. She must have suspected something there and prepared herself for what'd happened. She probably had been building up a resistance to him for some time. Well, he'd break it down. He had to.

"Annie," he said. "I will not let you destroy our marriage."

"There's nothing left to destroy. You can't bring back what you've lost and expect it to be the same."

"But nothing's been lost. You're making a big mistake is all. I'm not in love with Charlotte. I'm not having an affair with her. I'm not . . . "

"A minute ago you said you loved her. Either way, I don't want to talk about it. We never should've gotten married in the first place. I'm sorry to have been a barrier for you. I know you always try to do what's right, and I'm sure you're being married caused you some discomfort, but you don't have to worry about me. I'm not going to jump out the window or anything. I just want to be alone. It's something I'm going to have to get used to, and I might as well start now."

"Oh, Annie," Robert moaned. "Please give us another chance. We can be happy again. You'll see. I know I can explain."

Annie's eyes said it all: "It's over. You disgust me. Leave."

On the street below the hotel, Robert tried to convince himself there was some hope, but the vision of Annie's eyes wouldn't let him. Perhaps he still had a chance with Charlotte. He could say he'd told Annie the truth and they were getting a divorce. He and Charlotte could be together now. They wouldn't have to waste time talking anymore. They could fall into each other's arms like they always wanted. And now, there was no reason why they couldn't stay there. Over the past few weeks, he'd alternated between being borne along on a stream of love and being left in an eddy of guilt. In the eddy, he'd been spun against the current by thoughts of Annie and what his mother would say if she knew about him and Charlotte. Then he would battle his way back to the crest of a wave every time he went to Oaklands and be swept along again until he reached another eddy. But now that Annie had eliminated all hopes for a reconciliation, he almost felt as if he was on the crest again. Or would soon be. There was no doubt in his mind that Charlotte was a better match for him. Before his thoughts of Annie had ravaged him with guilt, he'd never felt closer to anybody in his life. At times, it seemed as if the two of them were one—a sort of married state of spirit and purpose that now made his marriage to Annie seem artificial and shallow.

But when Robert reached Oaklands, Charlotte wasn't there. She and the teachers had been transferred to Hilton Head Island to set up a hospital. The Department of the South was mobilizing against Charleston.

# XXI
## James Island

Six harbor batteries protected Charleston. To attack the city directly invited reprisal from all of them, and an assault on any one battery couldn't be mounted without suffering crossfire from at least three others. Because of its distance from the harbor, the landward side of Fort Wagner seemed to be the least protected. Only the heaviest shells from Forts Johnson, Moultrie, Gregg, and Sumter could reach the narrow strip of sand leading up to the garrison's south bastion. For this reason, Wagner was the most tempting fort in the harbor. Once it fell, its guns could be used in a siege against Fort Johnson, whose fall would enable the Union army to mount an attack on Sumter and, after that, Charleston.

But Wagner's apparent vulnerability was an important part of the Confederates' strategy. They'd gone to a lot of trouble to make the battery look weak when in fact it was the strongest earthwork fortification in the world. And nowhere was it more impregnable than on the south bastion. In addition to receiving the heavy shells of four other batteries and the full force of Wagner's guns, an attacking army had to squeeze through a narrow defile formed by a thick marsh on one side and the Atlantic Ocean on the other. At this point, which stretched for a hundred yards, any shell would have a devastating impact. Any bullet would find a mark.

A direct assault on Wagner's south bastion was exactly what

General Gillmore had in mind, but he wasn't so foolish as to let the Confederates know. His plan was to make the enemy think he was attacking Charleston by way of James Island. Once the Rebels reinforced Fort Johnson with troops from the other batteries, Gillmore would land his men on Morris Island and capture Fort Wagner before the Confederates realized what had happened.

But General Beauregard wasn't about to be deceived. He'd been protecting Charleston since the war began and knew James Island was the *last* place the Union army would attack. The general before Hunter had tried to reach Charleston that way and failed. If Gillmore wanted to keep his job as department commander, he couldn't risk repeating the mistake of a predecessor. Wagner was the only logical choice.

Beauregard wondered why the Northern generals hadn't concentrated on Wagner sooner. He'd gone to such lengths to make sure they would. And even then, he had to risk exposing a spy by having him suggest Wagner to one of Gillmore's aids.

When Gillmore heard the idea, he felt like kicking himself. It was all so obvious. Colonels Shaw and Montgomery under General Terry would make a diversionary attack on James Island, while he hid on nearby Folly Island with the main army. Once the firing began on James, he'd land his men on Morris Island and rush Wagner's southern parapet. And just to make sure there would be no slip ups, General Higginson would sail up the Edisto River and cut the Charleston-Savannah Railroad line at Jacksonborough.

But it didn't work out that way. And not because of anything General Beauregard did. The battle of Fort Wagner was decided not in South Carolina but in New York and Washington. A new draft law started it. The law enabled men with money to evade their military duty by paying the government three hundred dollars. New York's Irish immigrants, most of whom couldn't find jobs, retaliated with a march on the city's biggest draft centers.

Workers at the 46th Street draft office had just run out the back door when a mob of angry immigrants burst through the front. They destroyed records and furniture, but that wasn't enough. They wanted the building, too. So they set fire to it, trapping the people on the floors above them. But that didn't satisfy them, either. So they attacked and burned some more buildings and trapped some more people on the top floors.

Now they wanted blood. Only not from the rich: they were only taking advantage of the new draft law. And not from the politicians: they were only trying to raise money for the war. But from the ones who were responsible for all the trouble in the first place.

Most of the orphans at the 43rd Street Colored Asylum never knew what hit them. Over two hundred were clubbed, lynched, or thrown through windows. The oldest was celebrating his eleventh birthday; the youngest hadn't learned to walk. It didn't make any difference to the crowd; every child not hanging from a ceiling fixture went out a window. And those who survived that fall were stoned to death on the street.

An idea then spread through the mob like fire through a field of dry grass: murdering children had its moments, but there was bigger game to be had.

Christophine Simmons, Sergeant R. J. Simmons' wife, was the first victim. While her husband fought without pay in the Massachusetts 54th, she tried to keep her family out of the poorhouse by working as a laundress. Her first reaction to the mob that surged onto her street was to save her clients' linen. She feared it might be stolen. But this crowd was interested in more than laundry: the whole block went up in flames. Screams from within the buildings pierced the air, while rioters waited on the street to hang those who tried to escape. Some lampposts had as many as three people hanging on them.

The thrill of destruction and murder soon spread to other cities. Brooklyn, Jamaica, and Newark were the first to be consumed. Troy, Boston, and Philadelphia quickly followed. When the blaze reached Washington, Lincoln realized something had to be done. Soon. Over twelve hundred people had been killed.

The black soldiers on James Island knew nothing of this. For the past thirty hours, they'd been tossed about like so many corks in a bottle. Now, finally on dry land there wasn't one who didn't reek with the evidence of the rough voyage.

Nor did they know they were playing right into the Confederates' hands. While they did their best to look like a full-scale invasion force, General Beauregard prepared to attack with the army he'd gathered from all the harbor batteries except Wagner. If Gillmore found out what Beauregard was up to, the Yankees could bypass Morris Island and seize all the other forts without firing more than a few rounds.

Beauregard knew the risk he was taking, but he had little choice. The Union army was more than five times the size of his own. If he didn't route the force on James Island and prevent Gillmore from taking Wagner on Morris Island, Charleston wouldn't last a month.

The first shouts to reach the 54th frightened and confused the soldiers. Not the officers. They knew the Rebel yell and directed their men to form a line. There was no other defense. Terry's orders had been to create fanfare, not dig in. No one thought the Confederates would attack an army so much larger than their own. Obviously, they hadn't been fooled.

Montgomery also recognized the yell, and it didn't take him long to figure out how many Rebels were bearing down on the Northern positions. He didn't even try to make a stand. In the Second South Carolina, it was every man for himself.

When General Terry saw his left flank disappearing, he realized his Tenth Connecticut was in danger of being cut off from the transports and surrounded. If that happened, the entire regiment would be slaughtered. But if Terry didn't stay where he was, the 54th would be massacred.

Terry retreated.

The 54th pulled back, too, but only to fill in the gaps left by Montgomery and Terry. Time and again they rallied against the Rebels' crossfire.

Private James Wilson took it upon himself to attack.

Five Confederates wished he hadn't and called for help.

Several horsemen rushed from the woods, but Wilson dismounted them with his bayonet.

The Rebels then tried to challenge him with their bayonets while sharpshooters peppered his body with bullets, but Wilson would not stay in one place. One Rebel after another fell.

A company was ordered to take Wilson out of the action.

Wilson attacked the company. When his bayonet stuck in an officer's chest cavity, the Rebels had their target. Twenty rifles fired at once.

Still Wilson would not go down. He died with his hands around the throat of the Rebel whose bayonet ran through his body.

Trying to cut the 54th's line in half, Colonel Way's Georgia Cavalry was meeting the same kind of resistance. Way knew the Yankees had to be recruits; veterans would have run long ago. And now there was only time for one last attempt before the cavalry found itself spread too thin to resist a counterattack.

Way decided to lead the charge himself. He saw a colonel bracing his men for the attack and decided to take his head off. That would give the Blacks something to think about.

But as Way swooped down on the unsuspecting colonel, Sergeant R. J. Simmons leapt from the line, caught the officer's sword with his bayonet, and shot him through the neck.

That was all the Confederates could take. Under orders from Way's adjunct, they began to pull back. The day's fighting was over.

Now was Robert's chance to put some distance between the Rebels and the 54th. He couldn't run for the transports, however. That route had been severed by Montgomery and Terry. His only choice was to reach the southern end of the island and be picked up by the main fleet.

Making their way through the island's thick vegetation would have been difficult under the best conditions, but the rain that had been falling for two days took its toll. Sodden ground became swamp, swamps became ponds, streams turned into rivers, and rivers overflowed their banks. Flashes of lightning etched soldiers holding onto one another's coats as they tried to keep nature from succeeding where the Confederates had failed. Soon the path they followed gave way. The men found themselves in marshes where the water rose above their waists while copperheads and leeches had their way below.

Twelve hours and four miles later, the 54th reached the Atlantic. The rain had stopped and the copperheads were behind them, but they didn't feel much like celebrating. Colonel Shaw was dead.

# XXII
## Folly Island

CAPTAIN ROBERT SMALLS WAS STEERING HIS SIDE-WHEELER up the Stono River when he spotted bonfires on the southern end of James Island. He called for his longboat. If that scruffy lot was the Massachusetts 54th, he'd just saved himself a trip into enemy territory.

Smalls had been transporting Union troops since he stole the *Planter* from his master, but none were as dissheveled as the ragtail bunch that lay about this beach. And the closer he got, the worse they looked. Even the ones who were tending the fires seemed depressed and slovenly. Any Rebel with half a wit could have cut all their throats and not one would have cared. They couldn't possibly be the same regiment that saved Montgomery and Terry.

But they were. And their new commander, Ned Hallowell, seemed unable to take care of himself, let alone a whole regiment. Covered with mud and sand, scratched by branches and bitten by insects, smelling of blood and vomit, he was too exhausted to stand up and shake hands. And he was one of the better ones. Smalls wondered what was so special about the regiment that the Union army couldn't attack Fort Wagner without it.

That's what General Gillmore wanted to know, too. His men had taken all but a few hundred yards of Morris Island when the telegram arrived from President Lincoln: "Serious disturbances. Many Blacks killed. Massachusetts 54th to lead attack on Wagner. More instructions later."

Now Gillmore knew why the North had to replace so many of its commanders, and he wondered what other battle plans the president had changed. But Lincoln had his reasons. Whites were murdering Blacks at the rate of three hundred a day. If he didn't come up with something to thwart the people's aggression and get their minds back on the war, the killing might get out of hand.

The president found the spectacle he had in mind at Fort Wagner: the destruction of more Blacks in one battle than had died in all of America's previous wars. It sounded extreme, but he was sure it would work. If the Blacks could prove themselves brave but inferior in war, they'd no longer be a threat. Hostility toward them would be replaced by understanding. They'd become a race to be pitied again.

But the black defeat had to be followed immediately by a white victory. Otherwise, the plan wouldn't work. If Gillmore lost, too, the president would have done more harm than good. Morale would sink even further, and the little support he still had for the war would decline even more.

But there was no doubt in Lincoln's mind that Gillmore would win. He commanded over ten thousand men and, according to intelligence reports, only three hundred Rebels defended Fort Wagner. If there was anything to be worried about, it was a black victory. That would be worse than a white loss. And there was no guarantee the Blacks wouldn't triumph.

So Lincoln created some. He ordered Gillmore not to furnish the 54th with equipment to cut away obstructions or spike the enemy's guns, and there'd be no artillery men to fire any cannon that fell into the regiment's hands. The Blacks would have to attack without cover, maps, guides, or even a battle plan. They'd be given only one order: take Fort Wagner by bayonet.

Hallowell couldn't understand why the 54th was needed at Wagner either, but he told Captain Smalls the regiment wasn't going anywhere until all the stragglers were in and Colonel Shaw was buried.

Smalls asked why Hallowell wasn't having Shaws' body returned to his family.

"Too late for that." Hallowell pointed to a nearly naked corpse that lay off to the left. "The bastards stole his uniform. Can you believe it? Stole his uniform and cut off his privates. His insides come out every time he's moved."

Smalls walked over to where the young colonel lay. "Fiddler crabs," he told Hallowell.

"Fiddler crabs?"

"The Rebels didn't mutilate Shaw; crabs did."

Somehow that seemed worse in Hallowell's mind. At least the Rebels had a reason. Being eaten by fiddler crabs was demeaning.

"How soon do you want me to be taking these men aboard?" Smalls asked.

Hallowell didn't answer. The beach had suddenly come alive. Soldiers, who a few minutes ago looked like they'd never walk again, were running toward a man who'd just emerged from the woods. He was carrying another man on his back. His legs buckled from the weight, but he kept staggering forward. "It can't be," said Hallowell. "But I think it is. It is! It's Shaw."

The men swarmed about their colonel, cheering his deed and slapping him on his back. Robert wavered from the force of the blows but insisted on carrying his charge to the field hospital. What was left of the regiment's medical staff lifted the man from Robert's shoulders and placed him gently on the beach. One of them looked at the man's wounds. They were serious, but Sergeant Simmons would live.

The news sent a roar from the soldiers into the air, and the few who still had hats let them fly. Those closest to Robert raised him up on their shoulders. Their cheers sounded like thunder. Robert's eyes blurred with emotion as he was carried up and down the beach. Only when he was too weak to hold his balance any longer did the soldiers let him go.

Now it was the officers' turn. They pressed around Robert, each one shaking his hand and thanking him for having saved the regiment.

Captain Smalls also congratulated Robert and told him the 54th had been chosen to lead the attack on Fort Wagner.

"Thank God!" Robert replied. "Now we will wipe out the memory of Darien. Now we will gain glory for the Blacks and the country."

But the regiment was still a long way from Morris Island. Six hundred had survived the Rebel attack, and Smalls' only longboat couldn't carry more than twenty. If another storm hit before all the men were on board, the *Planter* would have to sail to avoid being capsized. The sea was already too rough. By noon, Smalls' rowers were exhausted and had to be replaced with soldiers. This enabled Shaw to transfer more men with each trip, but what the regiment gained in numbers it lost in minutes. The sky darkened and, with a hundred men still on shore, swells started tossing the longboat as if it was a toy. Those who weren't rowing had to bail; even those who could swim were frightened.

"Bettah we be drowned than saved by Johnny Reb," Sergeant Carney told his men.

An hour later, Carney wasn't so sure. Rain and wind pelted the *Planter*, and mountains of sea rushed to turn it over. Huge waves poured over the bow, tearing latches from their doors and stanchions from the deck. More than one soldier went overboard, but there was no going after them. Even if the mountains could be climbed, the valleys never stayed in one place or held the same shape for more than a few seconds.

Smalls ordered as many men into the ship's shallow hold as it could carry. He thought they'd make good ballast, but the sea tossed, pitched, and rolled the soldiers about as if they were so many grains of salt and Neptune was getting ready to toss them over his shoulder for good luck. Up and down they went. No one could keep his feet for more than a few seconds. Finally, Smalls had to admit he'd been licked. His only choice was to beach the *Planter* before it capsized.

Robert was the first to jump when the ship struck ground off Folly Island. If he could touch bottom, so could everyone else.

The water was only waist deep.

That was all the soldiers needed to see. Slipping and plunging into the black liquid, they waded to shore. Thunder crashed above them and lightning intensified the dark after each flash, but the men didn't care. They were off the *Planter*.

Robert moved them out before they could get settled.

The soldiers were tired and hungry, but after the storms, the Rebels, the swamps, the copperheads, and the leeches, the soft sand that tugged at their boots was a blessing. They didn't even mind when the dunes appeared. At least nothing was going to shoot at them or take the flesh out of their legs.

But nature wasn't through with the 54th yet. The sun broke through the clouds to turn the soldiers' wet uniforms into saunas. Robert was practically delirious. The last twelve hours had been living nightmare. And not just because of the storms, Rebels, swamps, and heat. If anything, they'd provided some relief from the torture that was eating away at him from within. Losing Annie had been a severe blow, but what he saw on James Island was worse. It was so terrible, it seized his mind with a thought that nothing could shake loose. What he saw, laid out on the sand waiting to be buried, was himself. Nearly naked, he lay with a cannon fragment in his chest, while nature did its work on him everywhere else.

Harry was right. Their lives were part of a cycle. Nothing was coincidence. Only Harry's mistake had been interpreting the cycle as a sign of some future greatness. It never occurred to him that he was reliving his life because he was going to die.

Now Robert's life had come full cycle, too. Each stage was as clear in his mind as if it'd happened yesterday. Just like his grandfather said it would be. In the past two years, he'd relived his entire life. His childhood at Brook Farm and his parents' involvement with John Brown at Harper's Ferry were all shared with Harry, who died at the same point in the second cycle as when he and Robert grew apart in the first. If Harry had gone to Europe and not become so immersed in the anti-slavery crusade, he might have lived longer.

And what happened in Europe that had been replayed since coming to South Carolina? Fanny Kemble. Not only had he fought on the grounds of Butler Plantation and talked with her former slaves on St. Helena, his insatiable craving of her had been resurrected in his desire for Charlotte Forten. And neither time was his passion consummated. All he'd ever done was kiss and tell lies. In Italy, he'd deceived his mother, and at Oaklands he deceived his wife. Both times he felt guilty. Could his guilt be the reason he told his mother so much about Charlotte? Did he really want Annie to find him out and punish him? The idea racked his mind for hours. So did a lot of others. Obviously he wasn't going to die at peace with himself.

Where had he gone wrong? He wasn't sure, but it had something to do with love because Fanny, Charlotte, and Annie were involved. And it also had to do with being afraid. Annie and Charlotte had both called him a coward, and his mother was fond of saying he was a well-known traveler on the path of least resistance. They were right. He'd backed into just about everything he'd ever done. Everything from Harvard to the China Trade to the Civil War was an escape from something else. But that didn't mean he hadn't done his best. He was, after all, commanding the most important regiment in the country's history.

Doing one's best wasn't the same as doing what was right, however. Robert had done his best to please his mother, Charlotte, and Annie, and they all thought he was a coward. But how could he be a coward? Hadn't he threatened to shoot Montgomery and didn't he carry Sergeant Simmons through the swamp?

The answer was so obvious Robert was embarrassed for having asked the question. He could lie to others easily enough but not to himself. Physical accomplishments were easy. It was just a matter of doing them. They didn't involve any thought or emotion. And what was the worst that could happen? Failure? Imprisonment? Death? He wasn't afraid of these things. Not in and of themselves. They didn't involve any loss. At least not to him. Maybe that was why he couldn't tell Annie or Charlotte the truth. He couldn't bear losing the love they'd given him. It was possible. Maybe that was also why he'd been afraid to declare his Unitarian faith at Neuchatel. The boys wouldn't like him. And he was right; they wouldn't have. But how did he know that? From what happened at St. John's, obviously. But he knew it before St. John's, too. That's why his mother had to talk to him so much about how bad Catholics were the summer before he went to the Bronx. The only thing he could think of before St. John's was when his grandfather had died. Maybe that was when his cowardice began. Maybe not getting love or having someone take it away was another way of dying. Something inside him was killed when Grandfather Sturgis died. Maybe he was afraid it would happen again. So whenever he got love, he tried to hold on to it even at the risk of being caught in a lie. Even at the risk of not loving anyone himself. He blamed Fanny Kemble for that. If she hadn't been so mean, he might have been able to love Annie more. But if that was true, why did he love his mother so much? Was it because no matter how much of a coward he was she still loved him? And would always love him?

He didn't know. The important thing now was to make Annie realize he'd been afraid of losing her love. That's why he'd lied. If she promised never to take her love from him, he would always love her. Now he had to survive the battle of Fort Wagner. He had to tell Annie the truth.

But that was impossible. The vision of himself lying in a pool of his own blood was too strong to be denied. And everything in his life up to now had been relived. Unless he could think of something that had been left out, he'd soon be stopping a piece of shrapnel and Annie would never know.

Robert went back over his life again, searching for something that fate had failed to recall, but everything was there. Whether he started from the beginning or the end, the cycle was complete.

Except for one thing. It wasn't much. Only a couple of years. But it had happened: Harvard. Nothing about Harvard had come up in the second cycle. He and Harry were students there and went to Class Day, sure, but that didn't count. It was the *events* that were important. If nothing happened between now and the battle that recalled Harvard, he would see Annie again. He had no doubts about winding up exactly like the corpse on the beach, but that didn't mean he would necessarily die at Fort Wagner. There were a lot of islands in the Southern department and the war was still a long way from over.

Robert played back his life once again. No Harvard. Then he tried to remember everything that had happened there so he could avoid repeating an event between now and when he next saw Annie. That was easy. He hadn't *done* anything at Harvard. Football, crew, the chorus, the ensemble, and Lowell. What else was there? Boredom? No chance of that here. Still, there was no reason to take unnecessary chances. Fate might remember something he'd forgotten.

# XXIII
## Fort Wagner

FORT WAGNER WAS THE ANCHOR BATTERY in Charleston's harbor defense. Protected on two sides by water and on a third by Fort Gregg, Wagner could only be approached on land by a narrow strip of beach known as "Suicide Alley." Soldiers attacking from this direction would be compressed into one large target by a thick marsh on their left and the Atlantic Ocean on their right. The alley, which ran for one hundred yards, marked the center of crossfire from Charleston's four harbor batteries as well as Wagner's two bastions.

And that wasn't all. Anyone lucky enough to survive the defile, still had another hundred yards of soft loose sand, several rifle trenches, a moat, and a complex network of traverses, curtains, and sally ports.

Brigadier General William Taliaferro was the man in charge. Known for his savvy and guile, Taliaferro had been doing his best to make the battle of Fort Wagner look like it was over before it began. The few guns he allowed to be destroyed during Gillmore's shelling were highly visible. So were the eight soldiers who died trying to keep their battle flag flying. What the Yankees couldn't see waited in shelters no bomb could penetrate: four ten-inch Columbiads, two smooth-bore thirtypounders, two forty-pound cannons, two eight-inch Navy shell-guns, one eight-inch howitzer, and seventeen hundred Rebel veterans.

At the entrance to Suicide Alley, the 54th also waits. The storms, the battle on James Island, the forced marches, and the heat have reduced the regiment's strength to just over five hundred men. They haven't slept or eaten in two days, and their only rest was a twenty-minute ferry ride from Folly Island. But fear is a more common emotion than exhaustion right now. Not the fear of death but the fear of failure. The time to prove themselves to the nation has come. Up to this point, they've shown they can survive. Now they have to show they can conquer.

Robert wonders if the Blacks will ever know peace. The half-bounty, the clothing allowance, the cut in pay, their fate if captured, how much more can they take? And now General Gillmore says that many of the soldiers' relatives have been killed in several days of race riots. He's ordered Robert not to say anything until after Wagner is taken, but by then there'll be some new kind of torment. And what will those who survive the war have to go home to? Poverty, discrimination, and death.

Robert wishes he knew the men better. As friends rather than as officer and soldiers. He knows many of them will not see tomorrow and wants to say something personal like his grandfather said to him just before he died. Something that will let them know how much he's come to respect, admire, and love them.

"Boys!" interrupts General Gillmore, reining in his charger. "I'm a Massachusetts man, too. And I know you will fight for the glory of the state. I'm sorry if you haven't had any food or rest, but the Rebels are tired, too. We've been shelling them for two days. There aren't many left. The honor of taking Wagner is yours."

The men cheer Gillmore, who tells them to save their bullets until they're inside the fort. That's when they'll need them most.

Robert thinks this is an unusual order, but he doesn't question it. Gillmore has drawn his sword and is pointing it at Sergeant Carney. "And when this man falls," he says to the troops, "who will lift the flag and carry it to victory?"

Robert's mind flashes back to Harvard. Professor Rawlinson is asking the freshmen class a similar question. Casper Crowinshield answers before Robert can get the words out. For seven years, Robert's replayed that scene in his mind, hoping for another chance to make up for the honor he gave to someone else. Of all the events in his life, this is the one fate has chosen for last. The only one Robert ever hoped to repeat. "I will," he tells Gillmore.

The soldiers cheer Robert. Gillmore salutes him with his sword and rides down the line. "I'll go in advance of the men with the national flag," Robert tells Hallowell. "You keep the state flag with you. It will give those in the second wave something to rally round."

The two men shake hands and part. The soldiers also say their goodbyes. Robert approaches those in the front line. He tells them the eyes of thousands will look upon what they do. "You must prove yourselves or die in the attempt."

Robert's cheek is pale and there's a slight twitching at the corners of his mouth. The signal for attack is given. As the regiment moves forward, the only sounds are the scrape of their boots on the sand and their hearts beating wildly. The way narrows. Shells from the harbor batteries start falling just ahead of them. No one falters, but the left flank is slowed by a marsh and the soldiers on Robert's right are knee deep in the ocean. Suicide Alley.

A sheet of white flame explodes from the Wagner. The light is bright enough for Robert to see what lies ahead. Or rather, what doesn't: no line of skirmishers is providing cover, and the ships that had been shelling the fort have been withdrawn. Then he realizes that there are no engineers, guides, or artillery men with the column. He hasn't even been given a map of the fort.

But he's getting a pretty good idea of what it looks like. Enough fire is coming from Wagner's walls to turn the night into day. The only attackers not falling seem to be those who have someone in front of them to stop the bullets. Everyone else is either spinning and falling to the ground or being blown up in the air by crossfire from the other harbor batteries.

Robert realizes that there are more than three hundred Rebels defending Wagner, but they don't stop the 54th. Or even slow it down. As one man falls, another steps forward to take his place.

There's no pause or check at any time. In fact, the soldiers' advance is so fast, the supporting white brigades are still in the defile when the 54th hits the moat.

Captain William Simkins is the first officer to fall. Captain Russell hurries to his aid and winds up lying dead on top of him. Theodore Tilton leads Simkins' and Russell's companies to the right of the southeast bastion rather than to the left as Robert has done. Those who aren't immediately shot by the raking fire that greets them run for cover.

But there isn't any cover. And the regiment following the 54th fires at the Blacks for retreating. Dozens are killed by their own men.

Robert, meanwhile, leads his soldiers up Wagner's south wall. The crossfire from the bastions is murderous, but they keep going. Rebels jump on top of the parapet and fire directly into their faces. So many men fall, those in the moat can't get out. One confederate, stripped to the waist, doesn't even load his gun. Others do it for him. All he does is kill. Every time he fires, a man falls back onto someone below.

Robert draws his pistol and shoots the man from the parapet. The regiment interprets his shot as a signal to open fire. Now it's the enemy's turn to fall.

Robert mounts the parapet. As the men nearest him fight the Rebels up close, he waves his sword to those behind. He can't see there's no one left to follow.

A flash of cannon fire etches Robert's figure against the night. Pointing his sword to the stars, he dives headlong into the fort.

# Epilogue

The soldiers who followed Robert into Wagner fought the Rebels hand-to-hand, but they were heavily outnumbered. Most of them died. The few who managed to escape back over the parapet had to cover the same hellish ground they'd just crossed. Only this time, they ran into Union bullets as well as away from Confederate ones. Those who reached what was now the front line were called cowards and told to go back and fight.

The first white brigade under General Strong managed to make its way out of the defile but no farther. When Strong died in the bastions' crossfire, his men lost their nerve. They fell back on General Putnam's brigade. But Putnam met the same fate as Strong, and his troops also demoralized. They'd hold their positions, but they refused to attack. Brigadier General Stevenson was the next into the defile, but the two brigades in front of him were retreating. Fast. All he could do was cover them.

What was left of the 54th was pinned down between the retreating white brigades and Fort Wagner. When the Rebels saw the main army pulling back, they rushed the isolated regiment. The Blacks fought valiantly, but they had no ammunition, no support from the whites, and were hopelessly outnumbered. Those not taken prisoner were given up for dead.

Sergeant William Carney was one of the few who survived.

He'd carried the national flag to the top of Wagner's south wall before fighting his way back to the Union lines. Told to return to the front, he waited in the no man's land between the opposing forces until the Rebels charged. The flag made him a natural target and he took bullets in his arms, legs, and chest, but he also picked up a sword and ran it through every Confederate who tried to take his flag as a battle prize. When the firing subsided, he crawled back through the Northern positions to a field hospital. At the front entrance, he stood up, cleaned himself off, and marched inside. The surgeons stared in disbelief; the wounded raised themselves from their cots and saluted. Carney told them: "Deh ole flag done never touched the ground, boys."

The morning after the attack, General Gillmore climbed his lookout post. A blue carpet spread over the beach. Every field officer in the first two columns was dead, wounded, or missing. Two-thirds of the men in the 54th wouldn't have to hear about the race riots. Neither would twelve hundred whites.

For the next few days, Gillmore watched the Confederates toss Union soldiers onto piles as high as fifty feet before dumping them into mass graves that had been dug in front of the fort. The Northern officers as well as the hundred Rebels who died were given individual burials.

All except Robert. His body, according to the burial officer, was "stripped of his uniform and thrown into a ditch with his niggers."

Of the hundred Union soldiers captured, sixty-nine were from the 54th. Twenty of those died from wounds. The rest were handed over to Governor Bonham, who placed the free Blacks in solitary confinement until the end of the war. The eleven former slaves were sent to Andersonville Prison. Of these, three survived.

The Union War Department tried to recover Robert's body but the Shaws asked them not to. Robert's place was with his men.

Toward the end of the war, Robert's inscribed sword was found in a Virginia farmhouse. A Confederate officer mailed Robert's sash to his family, but Private Charles Blake refused to give up the watch and vignette he'd stolen from the body. They remain in the possession of his descendants.

Francis and Sarah Shaw continued their support of the Northern cause. They helped form New York's first black regiment and, after the war, financed the reconstruction of Darien. The project was directed by Harry Russell, who hadn't died at Harper's Ferry but was captured and sent to Libby Prison.

Two months after the attack, Fort Wagner was evacuated. A Union blockade and continual bombing proved more effective than Gillmore's frontal assault. Charleston also fell, and the 54th led a victory march through the city. Before the war was over, the regiment was cited for bravery at Olustee, Honey Hill, and Pocotaligo. Ned Hallowell was appointed colonel, and Sergeant Swails became the first black officer in the Union army.

In April of 1864, Congress declared black soldiers equal to white ones. Eighteen months after they enlisted the soldiers in the 54th received their first paychecks.

Abolitionists saw Robert as a martyr and formed a committee to raise money for a memorial. Soldiers from the 54th donated fifteen hundred dollars; poor people from all over the country sent their pennies. Seven thousand of them. Augustus St. Gaudens, who was commissioned to sculpt the monument, envisioned a large equestrian statue like the one he'd designed for General Sherman in New York, but the Shaws objected. Robert had marched and died with his men. That's how they wanted him portrayed.

Sergeant Carney led sixty-five veterans to the unveiling in Boston. For the memorial's base, James Russell Lowell wrote:

> Right in the van, On the red rampart's slippery swell,
> With heart that beat a charge, he fell Foeward, as fits
>     a man;
> But the high soul burns on to light men's feet
> Where death for noble ends make dying sweet.

William James, Wilkie's younger brother, said the memorial bore witness to the brotherhood of man, and Booker T. Washington told those assembled that "the real monument to Colonel Shaw is being slowly builded among the lowly."

More than a hundred years later, it still isn't complete. Thinking about the city that produced a Massachusetts 54th and is still troubled by racial unrest, Robert Lowell writes:

Their monument sticks like a fishbone
in the city's throat.
Its Colonel is as lean
as a compass needle.

Shaw's father wanted no monument
except the ditch,
where his son's body was thrown
and lost with his "niggers."

The ditch is nearer.
There are no statues for the last war here; . . .
When I crouch to my television set,
the drained faces of Negro school-children rise like
    balloons.

. . . Everywhere,
giant finned cars nose forward like fish;
a savage servility
slides by on grease.

The Escaped Slave

AN ILLUSTRATION OF THE NEW YANKEE DOCTRINE ABOUT THE DARKEY.

CORPORAL —— MASS. REGIMENT.—Cuffee, advancing rapidly to the rear during an engagement, to Yankee officer, who tries to stop him—*log.*—"No, sah! can't go back dar—dis chile too '*motional* for dat sorter thing."

Page from the *Southern Illustrated News*

Negro recruits as seen marching up Beekman Street, New York City

HOW TO ESCAPE THE DRAFT.

Robert Gould Shaw

Morris Island. S.C. July 20

My Dear Amelia: I have been in two fights, and am unhurt. I am about to go in another I believe to-night. Our men fought well on both occasions. The last was desperate — we charged that terrible battery on Morris Island known as "Fort Wagoner, and were repulsed with a loss of 3 on killed and wounded. I escaped unhurt from amidst that perfect hail of shot and shell. It was terrible. I need not particularize the papers will give a better than I have time to give. My thoughts are with you often, you are as dear as ever, be good enough to remember it as ——

Letter by Lewis Douglass written from Morris Island

Charge of the Massachusetts 54th Regiment, July 18, 1863

Currier & Ives rendition of the battle at Fort Wagner

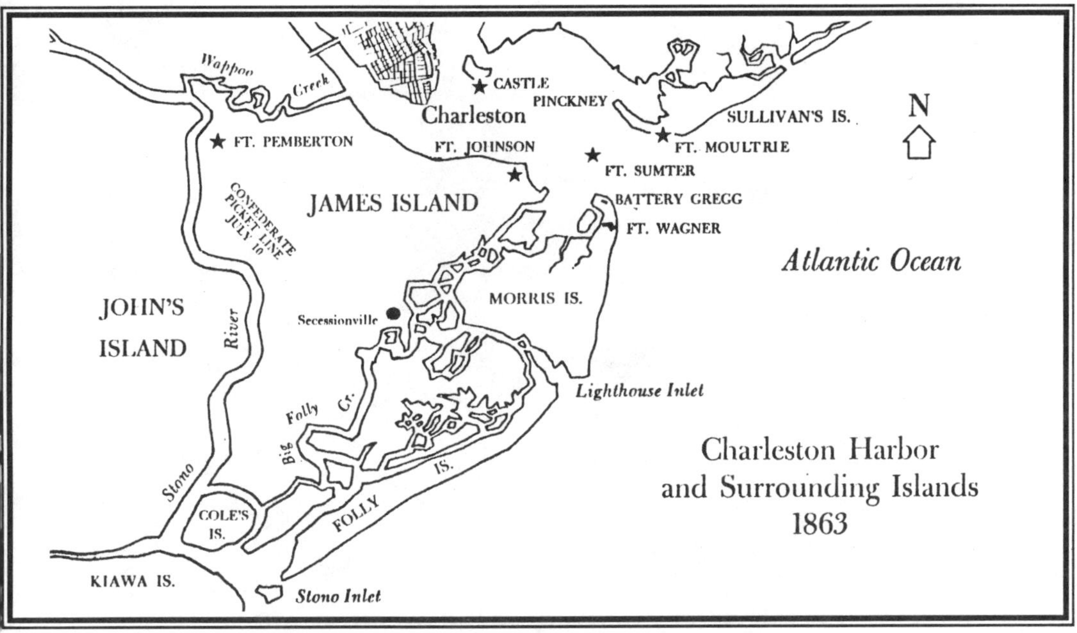

Charleston Harbor and Surrounding Islands 1863

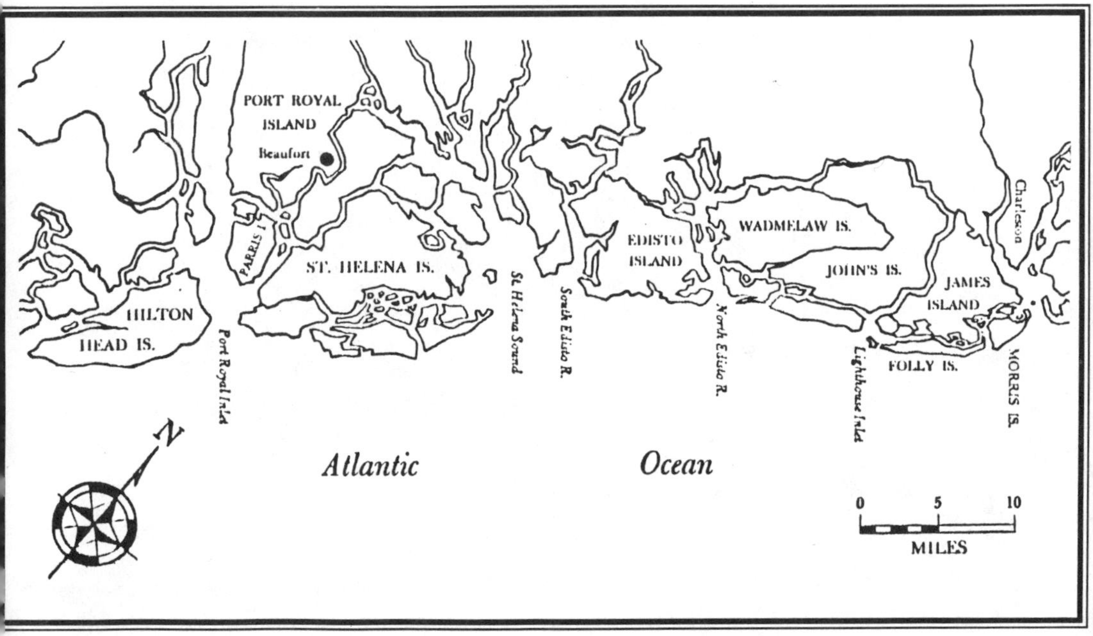